*She'd stepp[...]
She'd gone out feeling like a goddess.*

Now, Amanda felt hot, and hungry, and powerful. Using Scott as part of her burlesque act was like putting a torch to a stick of dynamite. She was ready to explode.

She wanted him. And in her current fierce state, she knew that for once, she was capable of reaching out and taking what she wanted.

She waited until he followed her backstage. People were hanging out everywhere. There were too many dancers in the hallway where she'd changed.

Suddenly, she caught a glimpse of a hallway, with a door marked Employees Only. She tried the handle. It twisted easily, revealing another hallway, leading to a service closet and an empty lounge, with another emergency exit beyond. The lounge and closet were locked. But the hallway...

Scott followed her into the hallway.

"Amanda, you were fantastic," he said, with that sexy voice of his that caressed her skin like mink.

She didn't respond, just smiled and reached for him. She grabbed his shirt, pulling him closer. He held her, stroking her bare midriff almost hesitantly. She pressed her breasts against his chest. "You're mine," she breathed, and meant it.

**Blaze**™

Dear Reader,

Ever sat at work, or in traffic, or just looked out your window and saw something so strange, you were dying to find out what happened?

Ever dream about having a larger-than-life adventure? Written down a "bucket list?"

Well, my hero, Scott Farrell, certainly has. He's heard rumors about The Player's Club, a secret society of thrill seekers in San Francisco. When he stumbles on the opportunity to join, he's determined to do whatever it takes to escape his boring life. But will he sacrifice a chance at love to join the Club?

This is the first book in The Player's Club trilogy. I loved writing about this secret group dedicated to living life to the fullest, and I hope you enjoy reading it just as much!

Enjoy!

Cathy

# Cathy Yardley

## THE PLAYER'S CLUB: SCOTT

**Harlequin**®

TORONTO NEW YORK LONDON
AMSTERDAM PARIS SYDNEY HAMBURG
STOCKHOLM ATHENS TOKYO MILAN MADRID
PRAGUE WARSAW BUDAPEST AUCKLAND

Recycling programs
for this product may
not exist in your area.

ISBN-13: 978-0-373-79666-3

THE PLAYER'S CLUB: SCOTT

Copyright © 2012 by Cathy Yardley

www.Harlequin.com

**Printed in U.S.A.**

## ABOUT THE AUTHOR

People think Cathy Yardley was crazy to trade sunny Southern California for the rainy Pacific Northwest. Fortunately, she firmly believes that writing isn't a job for sane people. Now happily writing in the wilds of Seattle, she loves hearing from readers. To do so, email her at cathy@cathyyardley.com.

## Books by Cathy Yardley

HARLEQUIN BLAZE
 14—THE DRIVEN SNOWE
 59—GUILTY PLEASURES
 89—WORKING IT
300—JACK & JILTED
332—ONE NIGHT STANDARDS
366—BABY, IT'S COLD OUTSIDE

To get the inside scoop on Harlequin Blaze and its talented writers, be sure to check out blazeauthors.com.

To the original underground secret society,
the long-running Loop That Shall Not Be Named.
Where else could I find an Empress
that gives a "fack?" I love you ladies: you inspire me
and best of all, you listen. Thanks for being there.

# 1

*WHAT ARE THEY DOING OUT THERE?*

Scott peered into the darkness. It was three o'clock in the morning on a Saturday. Most of his little neighborhood was sleeping.

Scott had been wrestling with insomnia for the past three months, which was how he noticed the strange goings-on at the closed Chinese grocery store across the street. Men had been showing up for the past hour, and disappearing into the alley. The funny thing was, none of them looked like criminals—unless thugs were starting to wear suits and ties.

There was definitely something strange going on.

He craned his neck, trying to get a better view, but the angle from his window didn't give him a lot of options. He considered going down to the street. But what if they were criminals, and they decided they didn't want some Good Samaritan type snooping?

No, he needed to observe a little more. From a distance.

Abruptly, he realized the perfect vantage point, and without a moment's hesitation he left his apartment.

Padding out into the hallway in bare feet, he opened the window and climbed out carefully onto the fire escape.

Now, almost the whole street was in clear view. *It'd be better if I were just a little higher,* he thought, then glanced at the fire escape stairs. The metal felt cold under his heels as he climbed up as quietly as he could. It was June, but it was San Francisco—which meant it was brisk, with wisps of fog licking at him. He regretted not throwing a shirt on, wearing only a thin pair of sweatpants.

There were only a few men going into the alley now: stragglers, from the look of it. He barely made out one man ribbing another one as they disappeared into the darkness. He squinted. One of them looked like…was he wearing a tux?

Who *were* these guys?

"Nice night."

Scott spun around. There was a woman standing in the open window behind him, wearing a large T-shirt with the slogan Well-behaved Women Rarely Make History. She was also holding a golf club like she meant business, which was at odds with the casual greeting she'd given him.

Scott cleared his throat. "I'll bet you're wondering why I'm out here," he said in a low voice.

Her full lips quirked with amusement. "It did cross my mind."

"There's something going on across the street," he said. "I was awake, and I noticed a bunch of people going into that alley."

"Really?" She took a step closer, but didn't let go of the golf club. "I don't see anybody."

*Oh, great, she thinks I'm a perv, some kind of Peeping Tom.* Scott winced. "I swear, there were a bunch of guys going into that alleyway."

"Why didn't you call the police?"

Scott felt embarrassment wash over him. "They didn't look like criminals," he answered.

"So you're saying, basically, that curiosity got you out on my fire escape at three o'clock in the morning?"

"When you put it that way," Scott said ruefully, "it sounds pretty dumb."

"You said it, not me."

Scott frowned, taking her in. She was maybe five foot six, with a thin build—her T-shirt billowed around her like a ghost. In the pale moonlight, he could only tell that her hair color was light, the length barely brushing her shoulders. She looked like a kid.

"You know, *you* should have called the police," he scolded.

Her eyebrows went up, and the golf club went down. "I'm sorry?"

"I outweigh you by, what, sixty pounds?" He sized her up, realizing just how bad the situation could have been, were it anyone but him. "I could have taken that golf club from you. You shouldn't try to be brave in a situation like this. If a strange guy is on your fire escape, you lock yourself in your bathroom and call the cops."

"Oh, that's rich," she said, her laugh tinkling musically. "I'm being chastised by my potential burglar on personal safety and home security."

"I'm serious."

"You didn't look like a criminal," she echoed, and

she sent him a wide smile. "The golf club was just in case I was mistaken. Should I call the police now? Or would you like to come in? You look a little chilly."

It *was* pretty cold. And the guys were nowhere to be seen. "Well, under the circumstances…but this really isn't a good idea, either," he pointed out as he clumsily clambered in through the window.

"Why not?"

"You don't know me."

"Of course I do," she said. "You're Scott Ferrell. Apartment 3D."

"Uh…well, yes," he admitted, momentarily non-plussed.

"We met once, when I moved in," she said. "About six months ago. I bumped into you and your girlfriend."

"She's not my girlfriend," Scott said automatically, then sighed. That response was getting to be knee-jerk. "That is, she's not anymore. I'm sorry. I don't remember your name."

"Amanda," she replied, putting down her weapon and holding out her hand. "Amanda Wheeler. Nice to meet you. Again."

He shook her hand, finally laughing. "This has got to be one of the weirdest introductions…"

"*Re*introduction," she interrupted, with that quick-silver grin.

"Sorry, yes, *re*introductions, I've ever had." She was cute, in a girl-next-door kind of way. Which was funny, considering she technically was the girl next door, in a manner of speaking. He shifted his weight from foot to foot, then glanced out the window. "I'm telling you, there really was something weird going on across the street."

"I believe you," she said, and thankfully it sounded as though she did. "Were you just planning on hanging out on the fire escape until the strange men came back?"

Scott rubbed his jaw. "Honestly, my thinking hadn't gone quite that far."

"I'll bet, or you would've grabbed a jacket."

He crossed his arms in front of him, then grinned when she giggled again.

"Would you like a cup of tea? Coffee?" She winked at him. "Hot cocoa?"

Definitely cute. "At the risk of ruining my masculine reputation even further, I'll take the hot chocolate."

"You can even have marshmallows," she said. "Don't worry. I won't tell anyone."

As she disappeared into the kitchen, he surveyed his surroundings. The light from the kitchen splashed out into the living room, revealing large windows—including the one he'd climbed into—and hardwood floors. The couch looked very comfortable, and the flat-screen television looked large, surrounded by piles of DVDs. There were also a multitude of books stacked haphazardly in built-in cherry bookshelves. The living room was cozy, comfortable and inviting.

Much like its owner.

After several minutes, Amanda returned with two mugs…and a robe, belted primly at the waist, much to his disappointment. He felt his own bare-chested state keenly. He took the mug, taking a sip gingerly so he wouldn't burn his tongue. "This is fantastic," he said.

She smiled. "The trick is to make it on the stovetop," she said. "Microwave just isn't the same. So, have the guys come back?"

"Not that I've seen," Scott said, deflated. He took another sip, savoring the rich, creamy, chocolate concoction. "What else is in this?"

"Nutmeg," she replied, with a slight shrug. "It's my own blend. I used to own a chocolate shop. Just sold it recently, actually."

He happened to be glancing out the window as she made her statement. "Look! There they are!"

The two of them huddled by the window, peering out. Like a colony of army ants, men streamed out of the alleyway, making the buzzing noise of people trying to be quiet and failing miserably. There were several loudly whispered mutters of "shh" and "shut up!" heard, and laughter, as the crowd dispersed and went their separate ways.

"It's almost four," Amanda said. "What *are* they doing?"

"I have no idea," Scott said, watching as a limo drove by and picked up several of the group. "Now do you see why I was out on the fire escape?"

She laughed, and it warmed him more than the hot chocolate. "I wasn't really complaining that you were out there," she replied, looking down at her mug. Then she looked back at him, smiling shyly.

He stared at her. Was that a come-on? After all, here he was, in her living room, in the middle of the night. In just sweatpants. And she was just wearing a T-shirt and a robe, from the looks of it. It could definitely be an invitation.

Of course, he had just invaded her place on the strangest of rationales. She could just be what she looked like: a sweet kid who was being neighborly.

He shook his head, handing her mug back. "I owe you," he said. "Thanks for the cocoa. And for not calling the cops. Although next time…"

"I'll be dialing them from the bathroom," she said. "Still, I don't think I could convince myself that you were a burglar. You're too…"

"Too what?" he prompted, but didn't need her to answer. He got a feeling he knew the answer.

*Nice.* She was going to say "nice."

He paused, his ex-girlfriend's words echoing in his head as if she'd just said them that night, and not three months ago.

*Scott, I can't possibly be in a relationship with you. You're too nice. You're too sweet.*

*You're boring.*

"Telling me to protect myself was really…sweet," she stammered. "You just don't seem like the burglar/rapist type. I watch enough *Criminal Minds* to know."

"Thanks," he said, then started to go out the window.

"You know, you can use the door."

"Oh. Right," he said, feeling like a complete idiot. He followed her to the door, stepping out into the hallway.

For a second, standing there propped against the door, she looked like less of a kid, and more of a woman, her leg peeking out from the split in her robe, her hair tousled and wild, her eyes low-lidded.

*You should ask her out.*

He waited.

Logic prevailed. The moment passed.

"Thanks, again," he repeated. He turned and walked away.

He just wanted to find out what the deal was with the guys in the alleyway. He wasn't looking for a girl-friend. He wasn't even looking for someone to date. He certainly wasn't interested in a girl-next-door type, es-pecially one who lived in the apartment above him.

And most definitely not one who thought he was "sweet."

THE NEXT MORNING, AMANDA stood in the candy shop. *Her* candy shop. It was closed for business, although she could hear some workers starting their day, back in the kitchen.

The keys in her pocket felt as if they were made out of lead. She tried to ignore the sensation, studying instead the artistic displays of truffles and bonbons behind the gleaming glass cases. Out of habit, she ad-justed a rack of dark chocolate candy bars.

A tall blond man stepped out from the back room, grinning softly at her. "You can take the girl out of the candy shop…"

"…but you can't take the candy shop out of the girl," she finished ruefully, tucking her hands in her pock-ets—and abruptly hitting her knuckles on the key ring. "Sorry, Ethan. Guess I was just getting it out of my system."

"Are you sure about this?" he asked, stuffing his hands in his pockets also. His normally placid face was etched with concern. "Are you sure you can walk away?"

She nodded a little more forcefully than necessary, pulling the keys out of her pocket and putting them in his palm. "Positive. Besides, I know that you love it as much as I do. Maybe more."

He chuckled weakly. "I have missed it these past two years."

She forced a laugh, too, wondering if that was a tiny jab at her. When they'd divorced, she'd forgone spousal support in exchange for full ownership of the CandyLove store. At the time, she thought it was because she was the one who had started it, a full two years before they'd gotten married. Now she realized it was to prove something. She'd kept it going, made it even more successful. Worked eighty-hour weeks to ensure that success.

She subsequently questioned who she was proving it to, but at least now she felt like the point had been made.

"So," Ethan said, jingling the keys in his palm, "what are you going to do now, with all your free time?"

"Sleep," she breathed, and his laugh sounded more natural. "After that, I don't know. Go on vacation. Do something exciting… What?"

She frowned as his smirk grew. "You'll probably read books and watch TV for six months," he prophesized. "Then you'll start another business. For as long as I've known you, Mandy, you've only got two speeds—workaholic or hibernation."

She bit her lip, irritated both at his observation and the probable truth behind it. "Maybe I'll have an affair," she mused.

"You know, that might be good for you," he agreed without rancor. Probably because he thought there was no chance in hell of it happening. He was probably right about that, too. "You need some passion in your life."

"Yeah, I think I'll hook up with some leather-wearing Harley biker," she joked. "Maybe ride across the country."

"Start hustling pool," Ethan added.

"Wear micromini spandex and do body-shots off of six-pack ab underwear models named Gunther," she said, mocking herself. "Really. The possibilities are endless."

"Well, if you put your mind to it, I'm sure you'll get it," Ethan said fondly. "Whatever else, Mandy, you're the most determined woman I know. I hope you get that adventure."

"Goodbye, and good luck," she said, giving him a hug tinged with mourning. Not for the relationship—she'd grieved herself out on that years ago—but for the finality. And for his comments.

What *was* she going to do with herself?

She smiled, a little crookedly. Then she hugged him goodbye and walked out the door, feeling oddly empty and colder than the sunny morning warranted.

"I'm late, aren't I?"

Amanda turned to find her best friend, Jackie, business-jogging up to her, her hair in disarray, her purse hanging haphazardly from her shoulder. Amanda smiled weakly. "I gave up the keys to CandyLove," she said.

Jackie enveloped her in a huge hug. "Come on. Let's get drunk."

"It's eight in the morning," Amanda pointed out.

"Bloody Mary breakfast, then," Jackie said, tugging her along. "And don't tell me no."

"Like I could," Amanda muttered, feeling a bit better already. They headed for North Beach, hitting Caffè DeLucchi. Amanda had the smoked salmon Benedict and the requisite Bloody Mary, while Jackie ordered her usual, chocolate-chip pancakes with fresh vanilla whipped cream.

"You eat like a kid," Amanda said.

"This from a woman who used to own a candy store. Besides, you live like an old lady," Jackie said, sticking out her tongue. "Food choices are emblematic of lifestyle. You envy my pancakes. Admit it. You *crave* my pancakes."

It was close enough to Ethan's observation—*you only have two speeds*—that she winced.

"You know," Amanda said, "I do sort of envy your pancakes."

Jackie noticed the change in tone and focused in. "What's wrong, *chica?*" Her expression turned murderous. "It's not that tool ex-husband of yours, is it?"

"Ethan is *not* a tool," Amanda defended quickly.

Jackie rolled her eyes. "You are the only woman I know who is still friends with the husband who cheated on her."

"He didn't cheat on me. He just fell in love with Jillian, and we split up so he wouldn't cheat." Before she could acknowledge Jackie's stare of disbelief, she shook her head. "And if I'd really loved him, I would have cared. That was the worst part, you know. Here is this guy, telling me 'I think I'm in love with somebody else, maybe we shouldn't be married,' and my first thought is 'thank God.' He dumped me, so I didn't have to be the bad guy. I'd dodged a bullet."

Jackie nodded, taking a sip of her drink. "I've suspected that. You were sad, but you were also sort of relieved. You just never said so before."

"I think I didn't want to admit it," Amanda said. "Now I think I'm ready to move forward."

"It will get better. We'll go out, party. Have some real fun. If I have my way, you're never again going to go to sleep at ten o'clock after watching TV for six straight hours."

"I'm not sleeping well lately," Amanda stated. Apparently her "rep" as a boring hibernator was well documented. She grinned, momentarily distracted as she remembered last night with Scott. "Of course, that's not all my fault."

"Nightmares?" Jackie said with concern. "Or just can't get your head to shut up? I hate it when that happens."

"Better." Amanda claimed her celery from her Bloody Mary, took a fortifying sip. "I spent some time with a strange man."

Jackie's eyes widened dramatically. "Oh, my God. Did you get lucky?"

"Huh? Oh, no. Not like that." Amanda quickly told the story of her visitor.

"I figured you've got a secured building, but you probably shouldn't leave that window open," Jackie admitted, then laughed as the story progressed. "He sounds hot, though. You should have jumped him."

"Yeah, right," Amanda snorted, finishing her Bloody

Mary. "Anyway, I was thinking of taking a vacation or something, but nothing sounds quite right. I want an adventure, you know? Ethan was right. I either work, or I veg out. I need to shake things up."

"I think that Mr. Window Guy sounds like he could shake things up," Jackie countered. "Like maybe your love life, or at least your mattress. You should totally sleep with him."

"What color is the sky on your planet?" Amanda asked. "Do you really just walk up to people and say, 'Hi, I think we should sleep together,' and then they just…do?"

Jackie looked askance, counting off on her fingertips. "It works five times out of seven."

"I've seen your data pool. No offense, but I wouldn't want to sleep with seven out of seven of those guys."

"That's because you think you have to keep them," Jackie said with a wicked grin. "For the short term, the results can be phenomenal. Even if they're not, it's *fun*. Live a little. When was the last time you had recreational sex?"

Amanda glanced around the café, her cheeks heating with a blush. "Um, never?"

"Don't knock it until you've tried it," Jackie said sagely. "You know, I think it's exactly what you need."

"What is?"

"A fling." Jackie's smile was Cheshire-cat wide. "Man, I don't know why I didn't think of this before. You need to have cage-rattling, bone-crunching, monkey-jungle sex."

"And another Bloody Mary," Amanda said to the waiter who was now staring at the two of them, wide-eyed. "Jeez, Jackie, what happened to your internal censor? Besides, I've had short-term relationships…"

"This isn't a relationship in any way, shape or form. You shouldn't even know the guy's last name. You just need to know that he revs your engine."

Amanda thought of Scott, wearing only those sweats, his hair tousled. Her heart was already beating fast at the thought of an intruder, but knowing it was her neighbor hadn't slowed it down one bit.

Oh, yeah. He revved her engine—and had since the first moment she'd seen him in the hallway, about a year before.

Jackie caught the look on her face. "Soo…maybe you should invite Window Boy up for some more hot cocoa. And other tasty treats."

"You're demented," Amanda demurred, taking a fortifying gulp of her refilled Bloody Mary. "I tried flirting with him; and he didn't respond at all."

"Maybe if you were Amish, that would count as flirting," Jackie scoffed. "Be clear. Ask the guy up, then ask him to get naked and see where it goes."

"And if he said no, I'd have to bump into him at the mailboxes, or in the elevator," Amanda said, even as part of her felt intrigued by the idea. "It'd be awkward. It'd be *awful*."

"You're a wuss," Jackie said, but dropped it. "So, what are you going to do instead? No vacations, but you want an adventure. What are you going to do? Bungee jump or something?"

At the thought of heights, Amanda shivered. "Not even remotely."

But the idea of an adventure—a *real* adventure—had her brain buzzing.

*Maybe that's what I need.*

"You could go to...oh, wait, you hate flying," Jackie said. "How about one of those Outward Bound things?"

Amanda hooted. "Do you even *know* me?"

"Girl, you are hopeless." Jackie shook her head. "You say you want an adventure. You say you want to be different. But in six months, I'm going to find you with a business plan in hand and you're going to be neck-deep in eighty-hour weeks, and we'll be back to monthly brunches."

Amanda swirled her drink around in its heavy glass. Jackie was right. Ethan had been right. It all depressed her even more. She'd gotten on this treadmill and it made her miserable, but she seemed drawn to it like a magnet.

*No.* She wasn't going to keep doing it. She was going to do something different...even if it was uncomfortable. Even if it were hellish.

She wanted to be an adventurer. No. She *needed* it.

"All right," she mused. "I'll ask Scott to dinner."

"Good." Jackie smirked. "Of course, I'll believe it when I see it."

"You'll see it." Amanda finished her second drink more quickly than her first. Then she stared down at her plate. She motioned to the waiter.

"Yes, miss?" he said, shooting a nervous glance over at Jackie.

"Give me the damned pancakes, would you?"

"Goody! You are serious!" Jackie burst out laughing. "Now, *this* is going to be interesting."

*IT'S A GOOD THING YOU'RE having trouble sleeping anyway,* Scott told himself as he scanned the street. *Because this is getting ridiculous.*

It was three o'clock in the morning, again. A few days had passed since he'd seen the random collection of men disappearing into the alleyway across the street. He hadn't gone out on the fire escape again, but he had found himself looking out the window whenever he was awake that late at night, especially when he just would've been watching whatever movie was on cable at that early hour.

*Too bad you can't be having hot cocoa with your cute neighbor.*

He smiled as he thought of Amanda—her makeup-free face, the billowing T-shirt. The shapely legs beneath it…

She was the polar opposite of his last girlfriend, Kayla, he thought as he continued to search the street for signs of the suspicious. Kayla was sophisticated, a sexual siren.

People often wondered how he could have landed a girlfriend like Kayla. Hell, he'd often wondered himself. Kayla's life was filled with drama—drama that he had usually bailed her out of, as he recalled. She hadn't complained about him being "too nice" then.

Not that he was bitter or anything.

Anyway, those days were behind him, he thought, taking a sip of his beer. He wasn't going to get involved with a woman until he was damned good and ready. In the meantime, he had this little mystery to unravel. It might be boring to someone like Kayla, but he knew that a puzzle like this would pester him until he solved it. And he was determined to do it.

Amanda didn't think it was boring. She seemed to find it amusing, maybe even interesting. He glanced up, wondering if her light was on. If she was even awake. She said she'd just sold her business. Maybe she had trouble sleeping, too?

He could always go out on her fire escape again…

*Focus, you idiot.*

He glanced down at the street, then abruptly held his breath.

They were back. He recognized the look of the men who were slowly heading for the alley, making their way to the Chinese supermarket one at a time, or sometimes two or three together as the hour grew later.

He didn't think about it. He threw on a dark sweatshirt and headed downstairs, his heart pounding with adrenaline. He didn't know what was going on but, by God, he was going to find out.

He opened the front door to the apartment building carefully, glancing around as he quickly dove into the shadows. He didn't want anyone to notice. He saw a man in a dark suit, his tie loosened around his throat and his top button undone, also looking around furtively. The man then turned into the alleyway.

Scott looked up and down the street. The coast was clear. He crossed the street, heading for the alleyway himself. It was dark, and smelled like garbage and Chinese medicinal herbs. Down toward the back of the building, he noticed light flooding out as a door opened. He headed for it, his eyes getting used to his surroundings. When he got to the door, he hung out, hiding behind a Dumpster.

A few minutes later, a few other men showed up. "You know how Lincoln hates it when we're late," one of the men muttered.

"Somehow, he'll live," another man said with a low chuckle. "Besides, I wouldn't be me if I showed up on time."

"Three o'damned clock in the morning," the third man grumbled. "Finn, can't you get George to change the meeting to some reasonable hour?"

"What, you getting old, Tucker?" the second man responded. Then he knocked on the door. It swung open.

"Password?" the doorman prompted.

"Luck of the Irish," the first guy, Finn, said. "Come on, we're already late."

"And whose fault is that, Finn?" the doorman answered. "They've started. Go on ahead."

The door shut, leaving Scott alone in the darkness. It was a meeting of some sort…run by somebody named Lincoln, or maybe George.

They had a password.

It was too cloak-and-dagger for words.

*It's probably nothing,* Scott tried to tell himself, as his heart rate started to speed up in excitement. *For all I know, it's some kind of twelve-step program.*

But his gut told him otherwise. There was something bizarre going on behind that door.

He wasn't quite sure what prompted him. Maybe it was Kayla saying he was boring. Maybe it was because he didn't have a lot going on in his life. Whatever the reason, he found himself at the door and knocking three times, just as he'd seen the others do.

The door opened. The doorman was a guy in his early twenties. He eyed Scott with suspicion.

"Password?"

"Luck of the Irish," Scott said, keeping his voice calm.

The guy looked at him, as if waiting. Then he said, "Come in. The meeting's already started. Follow me."

Scott's heart was pounding like a racehorse as he followed the guy down the long hallway. There was a door that had to lead to a basement. He heard sounds of a large group of people, and someone trying to call them to order. Scott felt the palpable rush. He was finally going to find out what was going on!

The guy opened the door, and Scott goggled. The place didn't look like a basement. The walls were paneled, and the furniture looked opulent yet obviously comfortable. It looked more like an old-fashioned men's club, the type where old rich guys drank brandy from large snifters and smoked Cuban cigars.

Many of the men fit that stereotype as well, wearing suits or obviously expensive clothes. On the other hand, there were also men who sported tattoos and looked like skateboarders. There was a group of guys that were bellowing like frat boys, and another group in conversation, laughing and talking.

What was this, Scott thought as he stared around the room, some kind of underground men's club? Were they gangsters? A West Coast Skull & Bones society? What, exactly, had he stumbled into?

It was around then that he realized the room had

gone silent—and that all the men, suits or skateboarders alike, were staring at him. Their expressions were definitely unfriendly.

*Uh-oh.*

He felt a hand clamp down on his shoulder. The doorman, flanked by two other guys, grabbed ahold of him and frog-marched him to the front of the room. "Hey!" Scott protested, pulling away, but they only held on tighter and dragged him.

"What have we here?"

Scott looked at the man asking the question. He was one of the frat boys—he was wearing a suit, but he had the drunken demeanor and too-loud, boisterous tone of voice that said he was half-bagged. His face was almost as red as his overly gelled red hair. He was peering at Scott with narrowed eyes and a sneering grin.

"He's a fake, George," the doorman said. "He got to the door."

"I knew the password," Scott protested.

"The password's a fake, you idiot," the doorman answered, but another man motioned him to silence.

This man was tall, with dark hair and a somber expression. He also had an air of quiet authority about him—something badass, although he appeared a refined rich guy. Scott immediately knew that this was the guy in charge. He must be Lincoln.

"So, what are you? A reporter?" Lincoln asked. His tone seemed mild, but his eyes were definitely gleaming with anger.

"Huh? No," Scott said. "I just… I live across the street. I saw a bunch of guys walking into an alley at three o'clock in the morning, and I thought I'd see what was going on."

Nobody seemed convinced.

"You can check my wallet," he said sharply, wresting his arm away from one of the men. "It's got my driver's license with my address, and my business card. I'm a sales analyst and researcher for Daventech." He reached into his pocket, handing the wallet over.

Lincoln examined the contents of the wallet, then handed it back to him. Now his expression became thoughtful.

"Off the top, he's telling the truth," the Finn guy said, his tone tinged with amusement. "How'd you know we weren't dangerous?"

"I didn't," Scott admitted, feeling more and more foolish.

"So why the hell did you come down here and try to fake the password?" the doorman asked.

Scott shrugged. At this point, with the angry glares of the crowd around him, he had no idea what had possessed him to follow his gut.

"I just had to find out, that's all," he muttered.

"Looking for an adventure, hmm?" Lincoln asked.

Scott studied Lincoln, wondering if he was being mocked. "I guess."

"That shows some guts. I admire that," Lincoln said with a slow smile. "So what do you think, guys? It's been a while since we've had a new member. Should we let him in?"

"Haze him first," the red-haired guy, George, yelled out, causing a round of raucous laughter from the men around him.

"That goes without saying," Lincoln agreed.

"Wait a minute," Scott said quickly. "I didn't say I wanted to *join* anything. I don't even know who you guys are!"

"Can you keep a secret?" Lincoln asked mildly. "Because if we agree to take you on—if we make you a member—then secrecy is one of the prime rules. And it's one we take very seriously." He sounded ever so slightly menacing. "Or, if you'd rather, we can escort you outside and you'll never see us again. No harm, no foul."

Scott thought about it. He still wasn't sure what was going on—but his curiosity still burned through him. He wasn't sure what he was letting himself in for.

*God hates a coward.* It had been one of his grandfather's favorite sayings. He hadn't thought about it in years, but it seemed strangely appropriate now.

"I can keep a secret," he found himself saying.

"Swear it?"

Scott nodded. "I swear."

"All right, then." Lincoln smiled broadly, and to Scott's surprise, the men in the room let out a barking cheer. "What's your name?"

"Scott. Scott Ferrell."

"Scott Ferrell," Lincoln said, holding out his hand, "welcome to The Player's Club."

"The Player's Club," Scott echoed, stunned. "No shit."

Lincoln burst into a laugh. "Heard of us?"

"Who hasn't?" Scott said. "Are you telling me that you…that *all* of you…are those guys that do all that crazy stuff? Jet-set all around the world, throw monster parties, pull amazing pranks?"

"So it would seem," Lincoln said, with a little frown. "We do other things, too."

Scott felt a bubble of excitement expanding in his chest. "And…you'd let me in?"

"Interested, then?"

Scott swallowed. "Hell, yeah, I'm interested."

Lincoln leaned back, crossing his arms, and smiled.

"Okay, guys!" George yelled, putting an arm around Scott's shoulders. "Let's haze him!"

With that, there was a loud cheer and Scott was grabbed and hauled toward the door.

# 2

"SO WHAT EXACTLY *IS* 'The Player's Club'?" Scott asked, yelling to be heard over the noise of the plane engine.

Finn, the guy who he'd heard say the password, grinned broadly. "It's a club like no other, my friend," he yelled back. "It'll change your life."

Nervously, Scott took note of the other smirking, high-fiving members surrounding him. He wondered absently if he were being kidnapped. Maybe they were some well-to-do cult. His stomach churned a little.

"Before we go," George shouted, with a slight slur in his voice, "we gotta go over some rules."

Finn rolled his eyes. Scott frowned.

"Go where?" he said. So far, the "hazing" had involved getting blindfolded, thrown in a car and taken to the airstrip with several of the Players. Now they were on a cargo plane, winging toward the dawn over Marin County. Scott wasn't sure what was going on, but at least they'd taken the blindfold off.

"Players *kick ass,*" George said, weaving closer. Scott could smell Scotch coming off the guy like fumes. The guy patted his pockets, pulled out his wallet and handed Scott a card—an honest-to-God business card, that said PLAYER'S CLUB on it in raised type. On the other side, it said George Macalister, Badass and Head Player.

"We do stuff that other losers only dream of," George continued, weaving slightly. "We play harder, we drink harder, we *spend* harder…"

Lincoln cleared his throat. Scott was aware that almost every guy on the plane was regarding Lincoln as the leader, and pointedly ignoring George.

"Here are the rules, as we originally wrote them down," Lincoln said. "Rule number one—to the true player, all life is a game."

Scott waited for him to clarify, but apparently it was one of those broad, sort of Zen statements. Scott nodded, encouraging him to continue.

"Rule number two—the game is played in the field."

"Not on your couch," Finn interjected pointedly. "Or on television, or on the internet, or your work cubicle."

Aha. Game as metaphor for life, Scott surmised. "Got it."

"Rule number three," Lincoln continued, "every day is a new game."

"No ruts, no routines," Finn clarified.

"Rule number four—players don't keep score."

"That means no grudges, and keep a sense of humor, especially with other Players," Finn said. He was acting as translator, which was good, since this stuff was about as clear as mud. "Incidentally, you'll want to put this on." He handed Scott a nylon jumpsuit.

Scott knew that asking "why?" at this point was proving futile, so he put the jumpsuit on. It was bright yellow. He noticed everyone else on the plane was putting on jumpsuits, as well. "Uh..."

"Rule number six," Lincoln continued relentlessly, "Players never lose. They just keep playing."

"Persistence and attitude," Finn supplied, as he strapped on what looked like a backpack. "Whether you're hitting on a woman or hitting one out of the park, we emphasize both qualities."

"Say, wait a sec," Scott interrupted, suddenly feeling alert despite the fact he'd been up all night. "Is that a parachute?"

"Yeah, it seems sort of lame," Finn said, "but these are the rules we came up with before our first jump. And, admittedly, we were sort of wasted when we wrote them."

"They *are* lame," George yelled, laughing raucously. "Screw rules!"

"Don't put that parachute on, George," Lincoln said. "You're not jumping."

George scowled. "What the hell? I'm fine!"

He was drawn away into a heated exchange with the jump master. Lincoln finished, "Finally, rule number seven—*keep it in the league.* You don't tell anyone outside the club about what you do inside the club," Lincoln concluded, his face stonelike, he was so serious. Scott was still eyeing the parachutes, but he nodded. "You don't tell anyone about the existence of the Club. Not who's in it, not where we meet...nothing."

"Anything else?" Scott asked.

Lincoln grinned, and glanced at George. "More a guideline than a rule," he said, shrugging...then nodding at the card in Scott's hand. "Players don't brag."

"Real players," Finn added, "don't need to."

Scott tucked the card away in a pocket, then looked over at the rest of the group. They were strapped up, tugging goggles on. Finn wore a wide grin as he headed to the door of the plane.

"You're jumping with me," Lincoln said, and walked behind Scott. "Tandem. Don't worry, this is my sixtieth jump, at least. You'll be fine."

Scott pulled on his goggles, feeling adrenaline flood his system. "You know, I have this thing about heights," he offered, wondering if he were making the biggest mistake of his life. This smacked of peer pressure.

*If all your new friends jumped out of an airplane, would you?*

"I figured," Finn said with a roguish grin. "You had that look about you."

"Don't tell me I'm going to love the view," Scott said tightly, his heart threatening to pound out of his chest.

"Actually, you're probably going to hate it all the way down," Lincoln said. "You might even get sick. I've noticed that cursing your ass off tends to help somewhat."

Scott watched as they opened the door of the plane, the pale early morning sunlight creeping into the hatch. The air was freezing cold, hitting him in his already queasy stomach like a cannon ball. "I don't know that I can go through with this," he said.

"It's easy," Finn said, and then yelled, "Geronimo!" and dove out of the plane.

The rest of the crew cheered—except for George, who was sitting sullenly by the jump master, his parachute on the floor, his arms crossed.

One by one, the rest of them lined up, falling out or leaping out of the open doorway into the sky, hurtling toward the ground below. Scott felt his palms go sweaty. He craned his neck to look over at Lincoln. "I've heard about The Player's Club."

"I bet." Lincoln didn't sound thrilled by this.

"Why do you do this?"

Lincoln seemed more pleased by the question. "Tell me, Scott. Are you happy with your life?"

Scott was momentarily distracted by the intensity of his tone. "I guess." He paused, almost squirming under Lincoln's accusatory stare. "Well, I'm not thrilled but it doesn't suck overly."

"And there's a ringing endorsement," Lincoln quipped. "When was the last time you were excited to wake up in the morning?"

Scott blinked. "I…I don't know."

"When was the last time you did something that made you feel as though your life was worth getting out of bed for?" Lincoln pushed. "If you died tomorrow, would you think, man, I'm glad I got all that work done? Or would you think, my life's going exactly the way I wanted it to go? I've got nothing to regret? I've done everything?"

"Who lives like that?" Scott asked, bewildered.

Lincoln smiled slowly.

"We do."

Scott processed that for a moment.

"Seriously," Lincoln said, "if you decide you don't want to join the Club, we'll be okay with it, as long as you don't tell anybody about tonight. We'll probably be changing meeting locations anyway, we do all the time, so we'll just vanish. If you don't want to jump out of a perfectly good airplane, that's understandable. Hell, that's *sane*."

Scott felt his stomach start to unclench. He'd satisfied his curiosity, hadn't he? He knew what they were meeting about. He discovered what he wanted to. Now, he could go back to living his life in relative quiet.

*When was the last time you did something that made you feel as though your life was worth getting out of bed for?*

Scott took a deep breath. From the open hatchway, he watched the sun start to peek over the horizon in shades of salmon and gray. The ground looked very, very far down.

"Last chance," Lincoln said. "Just stay on board, and you'll get dropped off at the airfield. Take one of the limos waiting there. It'll get you home, no questions, no judgments."

Scott waited a long, painful moment.

He pulled his goggles over his eyes.

"Let's do this."

He caught Lincoln's quick grin, making the guy look ten years younger. Within a minute, he was hooked up on Lincoln's harness. Lincoln told him what the jump would be like, but in Scott's hyper state, he barely understood a word.

"Okay, here we go," Lincoln said. "One…two…"

Scott held his hands out, feeling the rush of the wind.

"Three!"

With that, Scott found himself leaping out of the plane, with nothing but air whooshing between him and the ground.

IT HAD TAKEN AMANDA A FEW days from her brunch with Jackie to actually get the courage to ask Scott out to dinner. Now she stood in front of Scott's apartment, wearing her "sexiest" outfit—a white, eyelet-trimmed tank top over a breezy, silvery skirt, with white sandals. It might not scream "have-wild-hot-sex-with-me," but it was the best she could manage with what was in her wardrobe. She confessed she mostly had either business outfits, or comfy, grungy clothes.

If he took the bait, she thought anxiously, she might need some wardrobe improvements. Underwear—*lingerie,* she corrected herself—at the very least.

She knocked on his door gingerly. She'd decided the best approach would be to ask him out in the early afternoon, before he went out for the evening. She doubted he spent a lot of evenings home alone. She'd see if she could book some time with him during the week, like a Wednesday night or something. The guy couldn't be busy every night of the week, could he?

There was no answer. She knocked again, feeling uneasy. Maybe he wasn't home. Maybe he *was* home... and with, er, company.

This could be bad. Very bad.

*Oh, God, what was I thinking?*

She heard someone fumbling with locks, muttering incoherently. The door swung open wide. "Mm-mmhello?"

She struggled not to gape. There was a trail of

clothes from the door to the bedroom beyond. At least they were presumably only *his* clothes...

Then she got a good look at him and her mouth fell open. He was standing there, just wearing a pair of shorts. Did the guy not own a shirt? Not that she was complaining, but...*damn*.

"Um, hi," she said, biting her lip. His hair stuck out in cute angles, and his eyes were low-lidded, his skin flushed from sleep. He was good enough to eat—as if he'd just gotten out of bed, and would like nothing more than to go right back. She wouldn't mind joining him.

*What is he doing getting out of bed at one o'clock in the afternoon?* Even for a Sunday that seemed a little, well, unusual. On the other hand, not everyone was a morning person like herself.

She forced herself to focus.

"Hi," he said, his voice husky and a touch warmer. He stretched a little, the motion doing nice things for his muscles. She knew she was staring. "Sorry. I was out really late last night. This morning, I mean." He looked a tiny bit goofy as he sent her a crooked smile, and she couldn't help but smile back. "What's up?"

Her hormone levels were up, for one thing. And worse, they were throwing off her plan. "I, er, made a bunch of brownies, and I thought you might like some..."

She held out her bribe. Seeing his response to her hot cocoa, she knew he had a sweet tooth. She was armed with a dozen double-dark-chocolate brownies, with bits of macadamia nut toffee dotting the surface, interlaced with ribbons of caramel. She might not be sure of her own wiles, she thought with a small smile, but her sweets could seduce a chocoholic at ten paces.

*"Brownies."* He said the word reverently, his eyes going fully awake as he took in her offering. His stomach growled, and he laughed. "I haven't eaten since last night. Those look amazing."

She handed over the plate, and he quickly grabbed one off the top, taking a large, unapologetic bite. His moan of pleasure made her skin tingle.

"This is *incredible,*" he mumbled around a mouthful. "This is heaven wrapped in chocolate."

She smirked. "You should taste my Thin Mint milk-chocolate mousse pie," she murmured. "Trust me, it's orgasmic."

He paused, then grinned wickedly. "Don't tease."

The grin made her skin tingle and her stomach flutter pleasantly. She cleared her throat. "I was thinking of making one Wednesday night," she said, hoping it sounded casual. "Maybe you could stop by. For a slice."

There. If that wasn't suggestive, then she'd swear off chocolate for a year.

"Really," he drawled, taking a step closer to her, his dark brown eyes warming her. He was still smiling. "That sounds…nice."

She shivered. How did the man manage to pack that much invitation in just one syllable? Especially one she'd always considered completely innocuous?

"What time should I drop by?"

She smiled, feeling relief and adrenaline pump through her bloodstream. "How about…"

Before she could set a time, his phone rang. He let it ring once, twice, still staring at her. Then he cursed softly, as if he remembered something. "Wait a sec. I'll be right back."

He dashed inside his apartment, leaving her at the open door. She could hear his voice, saying a slightly grumpy, "Hello?"

She waited, her whole body alight. This could work. She'd lay a trap with chocolate, and once she got him in her apartment...

*What was she supposed to do then?*

She gulped. This required a little more planning. Jackie probably had a risqué idea or two to try out. At least she had a few days to...

"I wasn't expecting you to call me so soon." Scott's surprised tone broke through her mini-mental-panic-attack, accentuated by the fact that he'd deliberately lowered his voice. It was so strange to hear, she suddenly strained to catch what he was saying.

"What? When?" he said, sounding obviously surprised. "Yeah, yeah, okay. I've got the address. Am I supposed to bring anything?" A long pause. "Okay. I'll be there. And I'll clear my plans." Another long pause. "Yeah, I remember the rules. I won't tell anyone."

He remembered the rules? She frowned, puzzled. What rules? And why did he suddenly sound so secretive?

He came back to the door without the brownies, looking a little sheepish. "Um, sorry about that."

"Everything okay?" she asked.

"What? Yes. Sure."

He wouldn't look at her, and he was shifting his weight from foot to foot. She wasn't a master criminologist or anything, but was he hiding something?

"Well, anyway...how about seven?"

"How about seven what?" he repeated dumbly.

She felt the blush creeping over her cheeks as embarrassment kicked her squarely in the ass. "Um, seven o'clock Wednesday?" she said, hating the now-blank look on his face. "For the Thin Mint chocolate mousse pie...?"

"Oh. *Oh,*" he said, and now he looked embarrassed. "Um...something's come up."

"Oh," she echoed, hoping that she didn't look as disappointed as she felt.

"Oh, hey, don't take it that way," he said quickly, and to her utter chagrin she realized she probably looked even more disappointed than she thought. "I really did want to go. Do, I mean."

"Maybe we could reschedule," she muttered, feeling masochistic.

He sighed. "I would like that, I really would," he said. "But..."

"But." She cut him off. "Trust me, that's explanation enough. Okay! Enjoy the brownies, I'll see you around."

She turned to flee, to bury her mortification in hot chocolate...heavily doctored with Godiva liquor, or maybe some Bacardi. But before she could get two steps away, his hand was on her arm, catching her. Stopping her.

"I mean it," he said, and she could hear the sincerity, see the heat and truth in his eyes. He stroked her arm as he spoke, and she shivered. "I can't remember the last time I had an invitation I'd like more than a slice of your pie."

His voice was so deep, the words so warm that she reveled in it. That is, until her mind put together the double entendre, and her eyes widened to the size of teacups.

He apparently did the verbal math at about the same time. "Whoa. I didn't mean it *that* way," he quickly clarified. "I mean, I sort of... Oh, crap. I am screwing this up."

She laughed. "Actually, it was pretty smooth, all things considered. Sort of crept up on me."

"Well, normally I take a woman to dinner first, before moving up to the nudge-nudge-wink-wink stuff," he said, and she couldn't help but giggle. "The bottom line is, I like you, and I'd love to spend time with you."

She nodded, waiting.

"But this week is turning out to be sort of crazy," he said, dropping his hand from her arm. "I'm sort of mixed up in this..." He paused. "I've got a..." He stopped, looking frustrated. "My life has gotten a little complicated recently."

"Ohh-kay," she said slowly. *What the heck does that mean?*

"So my schedule sort of got filled up," he completed, looking miserable. "For...er, the foreseeable future."

"Oh." She stiffened. "Okay."

"But I really do like you."

"Sure." *Can I just slink away now?*

He ran a hand through his hair. "You don't believe me, do you?"

She shrugged. "I..."

He leaned down and kissed her.

She froze in shock. Then after a few seconds, her body reacted instinctively, ignoring her paralyzed mind. She kissed him back.

Not surprisingly, he tasted like chocolate and caramel and macadamia toffee. He held her tightly, and she smoothed her palms along his bare chest, loving the feel of all that heated skin beneath her fingertips.

The kiss was meant to prove a point, she felt sure. She wasn't sure what point exactly, nor did she care. As long as this chocolate kiss continued, he could be proving the theory of relativity and she'd just go ahead and let him.

His fingers dug into her hips, pulling her flush against him, and she let out the tiniest moan of pleasure.

Just like that, he released her, looking dazed. "Whoa. Sorry."

"Don't be," she said, her voice breathless.

"I just… I didn't want you to get the wrong idea."

"Oh?" She had no idea what the right idea was at this point.

"So, I guess I'll see you." He blinked, then shook his head. "Later. I mean, around."

With that, he retreated into his apartment and shut the door, leaving her standing there, completely confused.

*He's into something,* she thought. Something mysterious. Maybe even something dangerous. She wondered, abruptly, if it had anything to do with those weird nocturnal guys in the alley.

She started to walk to his door, to knock, to ask… no, to *demand* to know what the heck was going on.

Any man who took her brownies and kissed her really ought to have the decency to say *why* he was turning down what she was so obviously offering. If she were Jackie, she'd probably be taking the door down with an ax.

*But I'm not Jackie.*

She stepped back, then frowned, picking up a small white business card. Probably something Scott had dropped.

She read it. Then reread it. Then gasped as she put two and two together.

"No way," she murmured. "No. Freaking. *Way.*"

# 3

*THE PLAYER'S CLUB.*

Amanda savored the idea, holding the card in her hand. She'd heard stories about the secret underground society for a few years—from customers, friends, the occasional blog or newspaper article. Nobody could prove its existence: the Players were an urban legend who occasionally popped up after an infamous party or strange, over-the-top prank. They were suspected of hanging a Smart car off the Bay Bridge. There were rumors of the "Nekkid 5K" through Golden Gate Park. They apparently played tag on Machu Picchu, swam with turtles off the Galápagos, BASE jumped off the Eiffel Tower.

If she was searching for an adventure, this was one with a capital *A*.

*And Scott's in on it.*

She'd sat across the street in her car, waiting to see Scott leave. He had taken a cab, and just like those cheesy movies, she'd followed it, trying to keep a careful distance—although, considering it was two o'clock in the morning and there wasn't any traffic, she still looked like she was following him. She just hoped that he wasn't paying attention. She got increasingly nervous as his cab started to take her into the heart of the warehouse district, a confusing tangle of darkened, empty streets. Factories loomed sooty and vacant, silhouetted against the San Francisco nightscape. The whole scene looked like something out of a noir movie.

Her skin tingled. She couldn't remember the last time she'd been this nervous—or this sheerly *excited.*

She heard the music before she saw the lights. Pounding, driving bass and a throng of people. Her eyes widened as she turned the corner and found a warehouse, crowded with people. There was a bouncer at the door.

She smiled. Well, well, well. Seemed like Scott was going to some sort of rave. She wondered who these "Players" were.

She parked on the street, behind some other cars, and she watched as he got out of the cab and walked up to the bouncer. He said a few words, and the bouncer let him in.

*Okay, Sherlock. Now what?*

She set the parking break, then took a deep breath and got out of the car. She needed to be brave. She could at least ask what was going on, right? Maybe fake her way in?

She sauntered up to the bouncer, belting and adjusting her trench coat. "Excuse me…"

He took one cursory look at her. "Strippers in the back," he said, gesturing to the left.

Her eyes bugged. "Sorry?"

His deep set eyes narrowed. "Aren't you a stripper? 'Cause there aren't any women on the guest list."

"Oh, right," she said, shocking herself. "I just… prefer the term *exotic dancer.*"

He didn't crack a smile, and he still seemed suspicious. "Whatever," he said. "The door's that way, in the alley."

"Thanks."

She couldn't walk away—he'd suspect something. Of course, he already suspected something.

*What's the worst that could happen? You've come this far.*

She walked slowly toward the door, hoping to buy herself some time to figure out her next step. Maybe she could sneak in, sneak past. See what was going on. And then what? Volunteer? Ask to join?

*I'll figure it out when I get there,* she thought fiercely. For a woman who lived by planning and order, this sort of seat-of-the-pants thinking was boggling. Jackie, she thought, would be proud.

She was still mulling over options when she got to the door. It opened in a flash of noise and color. "Tell me you're a dancer," a tall, black-haired woman said. "I'm short four girls, and we're a packed house tonight."

"Uh…" Amanda swallowed. She'd taken a few dance classes, as a form of exercise, and she'd been on the dance team in high school. It'd been a long time since then, but it was an opportunity. Not what she'd expected—but then, none of this was.

*If you can do this, you can do anything.*

"Yes," Amanda said firmly. "Yes, I'm a dancer."

The tall woman sized her up. "I don't know you," she said, and she seemed as suspicious as the bouncer. "Who referred you?"

"I'm just working for tonight," Amanda assured her. "I overheard a woman say she couldn't make it at the gym, and I volunteered. I didn't catch her name, though... I want to say Millie...? Or Sallie?"

The lie sounded hollow to Amanda's ears, but she played it with a straight face.

"Probably Mitzi. She's always a flake." The woman sighed. "If I weren't so hard up," she groused, then gestured Amanda in. "Ground rules. No speaking to the clients. You stay on the stage or in the cage. You'll get a split of the tips afterward. These guys are classy, no dollar-bill stuffing in a thong or anything. You're just supposed to dance. Okay?"

"Okay," Amanda said, her pulse rate zooming.

The woman sized her up. "I'm Tina," she said, holding out a hand. "This is my troupe, the Bettie Pages."

Amanda smiled, thinking of the infamous pinup girl. "Cool."

"You're going to need to wear a Bettie Page wig," she said, pointing to a row of jet-black wigs on Styrofoam heads. They were uniformly shoulder-length and wavy with a straight bang cut. "And, of course, you'll need to get in costume."

"Of course." Amanda nodded.

Tina stared at her. "Now, I don't know where you're used to working, but we are *not* strippers. We perform *burlesque*. There's a difference."

"I know," Amanda said. "Sort of a Dita Von Teese thing." Her first chocolate shop location had been next door to a fetish shop, and she'd learned more than she ever thought she would. Which is how she knew about Bettie Page.

Tina's smile was brilliant. "Oh, thank God. I may be glad you're here and Mitzi's not. How about the black corset? You'd look stunning." She sized Amanda up. "Though, with a rack like that, you might want to consider the diamond outfit. Or maybe the tiger-stripe?"

"Um…" Amanda was struck by the choices on offer.

Another girl flipped her head up, her wig firmly in place. "The diamond," she said. "The corset takes too long, and we need somebody in the cage in the next five minutes."

*The cage?*

"Diamond it is. Here you go, kiddo." With that, Tina dumped a bra and sparkling silver hot pants in her hands, then walked off, speaking into a headphone. "We'll have a girl ready for the north cage in five, tell 'em to hold their horses, okay?"

Amanda took a deep breath, then sought the changing room. She quickly figured out that this hallway was it. There were half-naked girls hastily getting into costume all around her. She bit her lip.

"First time?" the girl who had suggested the diamond outfit asked.

Amanda laughed nervously. "Is it obvious?"

"Don't worry. This is the best gig you'll ever find," the girl said. "There's no groping, for one thing. The guys are all rich, and strictly hands-off…which disappoints a lot of the girls who go in looking for some side work."

"Side work," Amanda repeated, feeling slightly nauseous. She slipped out of her jeans and T-shirt, then replaced her bra with the glittery "diamond" one, a flesh-toned feat of lingerie engineering that made her full breasts look enormous.

"Tina doesn't approve. She's trying hard to push the troupe as part of the burlesque revival, but I don't know how well we're going to do." The girl sighed. "Sorry, I'm going on and on, and I'm supposed to be on the main stage in a minute. I'm Janet, by the way."

"Amanda," she replied, shaking Janet's hand. Then Amanda pulled the shorts on, and pulled on a wig. She checked herself in the mirror, then grinned. She could barely recognize the face looking back at her. Especially not with the impressive boobs underneath that face.

"Wow, you're stunning," Janet said with approval. "You're going to need makeup, though. Bombshell-red lipstick, don't forget."

"Oh, yeah," Amanda said, remembering the pictures she'd seen of Bettie. She quickly applied twice as much makeup as she normally wore, then added an extra coat for good measure.

"There are some boots over there," Janet said. "Don't be nervous, you'll be fine, see you out there!"

Amanda rooted around in a large trunk until she found the only pair in her size. Unfortunately, they were knee-high, lace-up, platform heels in a white patent leather.

"Hurry up!" Tina called, glancing at her watch. "I need you in that cage!"

"Uh, okay," Amanda said, hurrying with the laces. She took a few experimental steps. If she stayed on the balls of her feet, she could maintain her balance. Walking normally was definitely not an option, though. In fact, she noticed that the heels made her whole gait into a sexy strut.

She made it to Tina's side, who gave her a quick once-over. "Fantastic," she said, shoving her toward a door where the music increased a notch. "You're in the cage on the right."

Amanda looked. There were two "cages" suspended against the wall. She would have to climb what seemed like a twenty-foot ladder to get inside hers. The other cage was already occupied by a young woman wearing black lingerie with matching black boots.

"Go to it," Tina said, with another nudge.

Then, ignoring the men cheering, Amanda strutted over to the ladder with more confidence than she felt.

"Wow," Scott said, sitting in the VIP area of the hip club. "I didn't even know this place existed."

"It's really exclusive. Not many people know about it," Lincoln said casually. Of course, Lincoln did everything casually. He was wearing a tuxedo, but the tie was undone. He looked like George Clooney, or maybe a member of the Rat Pack. He was occupying an expensive red leather chair. "Ever since you found us out, we had to change location. I have a friend who runs this place, and he gave me a deal on it for the next few months, until we find a better spot."

"Why don't you have somewhere permanent to meet?" Scott asked.

Lincoln shrugged, getting up and pouring himself

a Scotch from behind the bar. "Some of us are trying to keep this thing a secret."

"I noticed," Scott said wryly, taking a sip from his own gin and tonic. "Sheer genius, hiding your website by creating a fake golf pants store, then giving us private log-ons. Brilliant."

"Thanks," Lincoln said. "One of our members, Tucker, is our resident computer genius. It's all his work—the only work he does anymore."

"Why all the secrecy, though?"

Lincoln's dark eyes bored into Scott. Scott didn't look away, even though the intensity made him uncomfortable.

"Let's just say there are certain parties that would rather not see us operating at all," Lincoln said with all the delicacy of a diplomat. "Reporters would love to write about us, and then we'd get all sorts of people wanting to join. People who frankly wouldn't fit in with our culture. Then, we get hit with lawsuits for discrimination because we turned down somebody who takes offense. What starts out as a friendly group of guys having some adventures turns into a bureaucratic and legal nightmare. And as you may know, the chief of police is none too thrilled with us, either. Some misunderstanding about a Smart car." Lincoln shook his head. "Nope. Better to keep ourselves the way we are. Quiet."

Scott chuckled in disbelief. "Well, if you ever decide to abandon all this, I'm sure you could get a job in the mob like that." He snapped his fingers.

Lincoln's eyes lit with silent humor. "I didn't always run this club, you know."

Scott couldn't help it. His jaw dropped. Wait, had Lincoln just said he was in the mob?

It would explain a few things.

Lincoln saluted Scott with his drink. "Enjoy the party," he said, his voice as mild as milk. "We'll want to talk business with you later."

He left Scott staring after him incredulously.

George walked up to Scott, clapping him on the shoulder. "Enjoying the entertainment?" he asked.

Scott scanned the huge warehouse. He knew there were men playing poker on the main floor. A few guys were skateboarding on an improvised half pipe in the basement. The music here on the second floor was loud, a remix of something forties-styled and jazzy, laid over a hip-hop beat. It was both classic and modern.

"It's a scene," Scott said. Finn joined them.

"Not *them,* ass," George scoffed. "The *girls,* man. The strippers!"

Scott glanced in the general direction that Finn nodded. There were exotic dancers placed strategically around the club. They all wore black wigs, they were wearing various types of lingerie or similar, and they were moving to the music in a very enticing fashion. Several were topless. The men who watched clapped appreciatively.

"Lincoln didn't strike me as the stripper type," Scott said. Lincoln actually struck him as a sort of hit man, now that Scott thought about it—ice-cold, supersmart, probably ruthless. He got the feeling that you didn't want to be on Lincoln's bad side if you could help it.

George didn't seem to share the opinion. "Damned goody-goody," George muttered. "I said, let's get strippers, and he got these chicks. 'Burlesque,' he says. No touching, no dollar-stuffing. What the hell's the point of *that?*" He shook his head. "Lincoln might've started this club with my little cousin Finn, but trust me, it sucked until *I* got here."

Scott saw that several of the dancers were doing the usual strip-club moves, each bump and grind deliberate and blatantly sexual. There were others who were being more artistic about it, he noticed. One woman did a fan dance as she stripped out of her halter top, only showing flashes of skin. Another used her top hat as a sort of tease.

*Whatever.* He waited until George had moved on to another bunch of rowdy guys, drinking at the bar, then started to head away. He could see strippers anywhere. The Player's Club had a reputation for high risk. *Adventure.*

He was here for that.

A glimmer of light caught his eye, and for the first time he noticed that high on the wall, there were two cages set up, with yet two more dancers performing from their high perches. One woman was moving confidently. The other, he noticed, was a bit out of her element.

No—she was downright uncomfortable. It probably beat the hell out of stripping at a sleazy club, but she still didn't seem too enthusiastic. She was swaying lightly, barely shimmying. Men were hooting and catcalling at her, making fun of her lackluster performance.

He wasn't sure what prompted him to walk toward her—to defend her, maybe, or help her leave. By the time he got there, however, the crowd's reaction to her had prompted her to step up her routine a little. Scott looked up to see her moving with an almost aggressive enthusiasm. The crowd's whistles and hooting were now appreciative. Even the other dancing girl seemed taken by surprise.

The woman planted her legs in an inverted V, leaning heavily at her waist, her full breasts put on prominent display—and quite a display it was, Scott had to admit. With a scooping, undulating motion, she stretched up and turned, her panties displaying a very shapely backside. She did another quick shimmy, and the guys were riveted. She then reached back gracefully with one hand and reached for the clasp of her bra top.

The men surrounding Scott were clapping and shouting. Scott had never really been a fan of strippers—he was definitely a fan of naked women—but this woman was definitely appealing. She unhooked the clasp, then turned around, crossing her arms in front of her to catch the falling garment. Her pouty, red-painted mouth made an O of surprise, which she then covered with one hand. She looked like the ultimate naughty girl.

The crowd roared, and she broke character to smile back at them—a full, delighted smile.

His eyes narrowed.

*I know that smile.*

Where the hell had he seen her before?

It wasn't like he knew a lot of dancers, exotic or otherwise. He watched with the scrutiny of a federal investigator as she twirled and danced, never completely baring anything, putting the *tease* in striptease. When she rehooked her bra and started to exit the cage, she had the assembled men eating out of her hand. Scott was still unsure of her identity, but he knew right down in his bones that he'd seen that smile before, and he was suddenly compelled to find out who this exotic, amazing woman might be.

She descended the ladder, making her way through the crowd that was obviously captivated by her, smiling and laughing with the dancer that was replacing her.

Then her eyes met Scott's. They widened, a pale, almost silvery blue-gray, large and luminous.

She smiled. Then slowly, deliberately, she motioned him to follow her.

AMANDA HAD NEVER FELT like this before. Climbing into the cage, she'd felt like an idiot, an impostor. A fool. She couldn't copy the stripper gyrations of the woman in the cage next to her. But after a few minutes, with the men jeering and catcalling, something in her just snapped. She remembered the film *Gypsy*. Somehow, she channeled the playfulness of Natalie Wood with the statuesque beauty of Bettie Page herself.

She'd stepped in feeling like a fool. She'd gone out feeling like a goddess.

Now she felt hot and hungry and powerful. Seeing Scott was like putting a torch to a stick of dynamite. She was ready to explode.

She wanted him. And in her current fierce state, she knew that for once, she was capable of reaching out and taking what she wanted.

She waited until he followed her, and her eyes scanned the building. Men were hanging out everywhere. There were too many dancers in the hallway where she'd changed.

Suddenly, she caught a glimpse of a hallway with a door marked Employees Only. She tried the handle. It twisted easily, revealing another hallway, leading to a service closet and an empty lounge with another emergency exit beyond. The lounge and closet were both locked. But the hallway...would do.

Scott was right behind her.

"Hi," he said with that sexy voice of his that caressed her skin like mink.

She didn't respond, just smiled and reached for him. She grabbed his shirt, pulling him closer. He reached out, stroking her bare midriff almost hesitantly. She pressed her breasts against his chest.

He groaned, and then his body pressed her against the wall. A man's raucous laugh sounded just beyond the door. Half laughing, she tugged him farther along the hallway to an alcove half-filled with boxes, tucked away from any passersby. It was no more than a nook—but it was dark, and more important, it was private.

She stood on her toes, rubbing her pelvis against his, and she kissed him.

She could feel his cock already straining against the fabric of his pants, prodding her like a length of hard, hot steel. A nice length, she thought with approval. She went immediately wet. His fingers dug into her hips, pulling her flush against him, caressing her. His mouth opened, forcing hers to follow suit. They kissed, tasting and testing, his tongue moving forward. She tangled hers with his, stroking it as her nipples went hard, the diamonds of her bra scratching against his shirt.

"I want you," she breathed.

"You are so sexy," he murmured back, against her lips. He moved, pressing hot, nipping kisses along her neck, causing her to gasp and shiver against him, one leg moving to caress his leg, her knee hooking on his hip. "You're the most beautiful woman I've ever seen."

She whimpered when one hand smoothed down her stomach…then reached between her legs, pressing where she most needed pressure.

"Scott," she said, her head falling back.

His hand froze at the juncture of her thighs. "What?"

She had trouble focusing, but realized he was staring at her. "What?" she echoed, still drowning in sensation.

"How do you know me?"

She didn't want to talk. Didn't want to reason. She clutched his hand with her thighs, arching her back so her breasts pressed hard against his chest. He groaned involuntarily, his fingers moving to push her rock-hard clit. She wanted to cry with pleasure. She wanted to strip down, get him inside her.

He moved his hand away, slowly, reluctantly. "How do you know me?" he asked again, more insistently.

She sighed. Then, reaching up, she took off the Bettie Page wig and hair stocking, letting her blond hair fall down.

He stared at her for a long moment, and she felt the buzz start to subside as that feeling of foolishness, of being an impostor, came back.

"Amanda?"

She nodded, tilting her chin up defiantly.

His eyes smoldered. Then he leaned in, kissing her with even more intensity.

She cried out against his mouth as he crushed her against the wall. Her legs parted, making room for him. He reached down, lifting both legs up, guiding them around his waist as his hips started to rock, slowly and intently, against her core.

He cupped her breasts, massaging them gently, fanning the flames of her already incandescent need. She twisted, slow and deliberate, against his erection.

"I want you now," she said, biting his earlobe. "I want to feel you."

He shuddered against her. "Baby," he said, and his thumbs dipped below the bra, dragging over her rock-hard nipples and making her gasp raggedly. "I am so hard for you."

She was on fire. She was going to die. She clawed at his shoulders. "Take my pants off."

He paused. "What?"

"My pants," she rasped. "Take them off."

He released her. She put her platform heels on the floor, and he reached for the snap on her pants. He paused again.

"Do you have a condom?"

She didn't want to think about that. Didn't care.

*Be reasonable.*

She shook her head.

He put his forehead gently against hers, and for a second, all they could hear was the muted thudding of the music from the club, and the scratchy, uneven sound of their breathing. He kissed her again, long and hard.

And released the closure on her pants.

"I've got condoms at my apartment," she said. "Or… there's got to be a convenience store somewhere…"

He stroked her breasts, her hips, kissing her shoulders, her neck, her jawline. "Okay. Let's—"

The door at the end of the hallway opened. "Yo! Scott! Pledge Scott, you here? Because if your ass isn't up in the VIP room in about two minutes, your ass is *out* of the Club!"

The door shut with a slam.

She glanced at him, curiously.

"I…"

She smiled, putting a finger to his lips…wiping off the lipstick that had smeared around that gorgeous mouth of his. "Shh. It's all right."

"I hurt, I want you so badly," he said.

It made her shudder and moan softly.

"My window," she said.

He frowned.

"You know where to find me," she whispered, then turned and walked away on shaky legs.

# 4

"NICE OF YOU TO JOIN US," Lincoln drawled.

Scott quickly sat where Lincoln told him to, in front of the crowd of guys. The dancers had left, he noticed...and thinking of the dancers immediately made him think of Amanda.

Amanda, the neighbor.

Amanda, the dancer. The striptease artist.

The girl who had offered him a slice of pie, and then quite a bit more.

*Girl next door, my ass!*

Scott shook his head, forcing himself to focus. Considering he'd already been "hazed" with skydiving, he wasn't quite sure what they were expecting him to do next. Walk over fire?

"We always start easy," Lincoln said.

"Gawd," George heckled from the bar. "The questions? Really?"

Lincoln silenced him with a cold stare. The rest of the rowdy crowd quieted.

*When Lincoln talks, people listen.* What was George doing with this crew, anyway?

"Easy," Lincoln repeated, this time with more of an edge. "Just getting to know you. What do you do for a living, Scott?"

"I'm an analyst," he said. "I crunch numbers. Forecast. Stuff like that." *Boring stuff like that,* he amended mentally.

"Ah-ah-ah-*nerd!*" George pretended to sneeze, causing a few drunken guffaws from the guys surrounding him.

Lincoln looked at the ceiling, as if praying for patience. "Let's pose a hypothetical," he said, ignoring George. "You have, say, a month left to live. What would you wish you'd done? What would you regret not doing?"

Scott blinked. "I don't know. Haven't really thought about it, I guess."

"Well, don't think about it too much," Lincoln said. "Just spit out the first three things that come to mind."

Scott frowned. "Sort of a bucket list thing?"

"Sure. Whatever."

"All right." Scott took a deep breath. "I've always wanted to do one of those spirit quest things. You know, where you go out to the desert by yourself and just be with nature."

He'd barely finished the sentence before George blew a loud raspberry. "Lame!"

"Damn it, George," Lincoln snarled, turning to the guy and advancing on him. George actually retreated a little. "Be quiet, or wait outside."

"You can't kick me out," George said, but he looked quickly at his posse, taking courage from their numbers.

"Try me." Lincoln's voice was low, and his hands were bunched in fists.

George quieted, even as several of his friends glared at Lincoln.

"Sorry, where were we?" Lincoln said. "What else would you do, Scott?"

Scott swallowed hard. George was a jerk, but he had to admit—this was The Player's Club, not the Self-realization Fellowship. He needed to impress them.

*What would a Player want to do?* He racked his brain, thinking of the shady rumors he'd read about them. They liked playing pranks. He sucked at pranks. They went on large-scale adventures.

They partied like rock stars…

"I'd, uh, want to crash a huge party," he said. "Like, something epic."

He could've sworn Lincoln looked disappointed. The frat boy contingent at the bar, however, hooted with approval.

"Anything else?" Lincoln said.

He took a deep breath. What was he missing?

He closed his eyes, trying to think of what he'd do, if he really knew he was dying. If he wanted to have one last, memorable adventure.

*What would a nonboring person want to do?*

"I'd…I'd run with the bulls. In Pamplona."

Lincoln seemed solemn. Then, slowly, he smiled.

The rest of the room started murmuring and chuckling, punching each other on the shoulder.

"Do I need to add anything more?" Scott asked, his mind still racing for alternatives.

"No, that ought to do it," Lincoln said. "All right. He's got his three."

Scott squinted at him. "What do you mean, my three?"

"In the next month," Lincoln said, smiling, "you need to do a vision quest in the Mojave, crash a really epic party and run with the bulls in Pamplona."

"Lucky thing it's in July," Finn noted. "Good choice, by the way. We haven't been there in, what, two years?"

"At least," Lincoln agreed.

"How am I supposed to do that?" Scott gaped.

"Don't worry," Finn said, clapping a hand on his shoulder. "We'll help. Part of being a Player is helping the pledges. Especially when they've got cool challenges."

"Yeah, nobody wanted to help me when I said I'd write a novel," another guy grumbled.

"You guys are like old ladies," George said with a swagger. "Me 'n' the boys are gonna go find some after-hours fun, since you kicked the strippers out."

"Fine," Lincoln said without looking at him.

"Hey, cuz?" George nudged Finn hard. "Tell your boyfriend not to be so damned touchy."

With another raucous burst of laughter, George and about six of the guys left.

Lincoln sighed. "Finn…"

"I know," Finn said. "He doesn't mean it."

"He printed up *business cards*." Lincoln grimaced. "I know he's your cousin, but…"

"I'll talk to him." With that, Finn trotted out.

"What's up with them?"

"Finn and I started this club," Lincoln said, shrugging. "It's a long story but, basically, we brought George on kind of early. Let's just say he has a different vision for the club."

"Tappa Kegga Beer meets *Bachelor Party?*" Scott observed.

"Exactly. Anyway, it's important that you don't tell *anyone,*" Lincoln said. "They'll kick you out for less. And I hate to say, but some of the club can be sort of vindictive if they think you've used the Club as a way to impress people."

"Unless you're one of George's crew," Tucker said.

"Not a problem." Scott didn't want to be part of George's crew.

"And you need to complete the challenges in the time frame," Lincoln finished.

"I know somebody who runs Vision Quests," a short guy with a pencil-thin mustache said. "Give me your email, I'll shoot you his website."

"Great."

"And you're going to have a list of people who want to go to Pamplona," Lincoln said, grinning. "I'll be there, myself."

"What about the party?"

Lincoln eyed the remaining Players. They laughed.

"Think you're on your own with that one," Lincoln said. "If you wanted to BASE jump from the Hoover Dam, we know people. Crashing a party isn't really my bag."

Tucker ran his tongue around his teeth. "Maybe George has some suggestions."

"I'll manage," Scott said quickly, causing more laughter.

"All right. Next meeting's in a week, same time, same place. And again," Lincoln said sharply. "Don't. Tell. *Anyone.*"

Scott headed back out to his car, cold, tired and a little blown away. He had one month to go camping out in the Mojave. Crash an epic party. And run with the bulls in Pamplona.

After his skydiving jaunt last weekend.

His life had suddenly gotten exponentially more interesting. *Who's the nice guy now, Kayla?*

He glanced at his watch. Three in the morning, and he still had a ways to get home. He yawned. He could really use some sleep.

Then, as he climbed into his Chevy, he remembered.

Amanda was at home. Waiting for him. Window open.

He had another adventure waiting. Wide-awake, he hit the gas and screeched out of the parking lot.

AT THREE-FORTY, AMANDA finally fell into a fitful, restless sleep. It had taken about an hour to finally calm down. The mental images of what she'd done buzzed around in her head, surreal, like remembering a vivid dream.

She'd stalked a neighbor to a seedy club in the industrial district.

Sneaked in with a lie.

Danced half-naked in a cage.

*Practically had sex in an out-of-the-way corner...*

She shivered. She wasn't sure if she was shocked, appalled...or thrilled.

Tossing one way then the other, she imagined that the bed dipped slightly. A man's weight. She tensed in reflex.

Then sighed.

Breathing deeply, she smelled Scott's scent—a light mix of sandalwood-inspired cologne and a clean, masculine aroma that she imagined she could become addicted to. She curled, imagining his warmth at her back...the heavy, probing feel of his cock, smoothing against her back legs. She moaned softly, yearning.

His hands roamed over her hips as he nibbled on the back of her neck. By the time he'd sucked a hot kiss where her neck met her collarbone, his hands had finally discovered her breasts, kneading them gently.

Her moan was more insistent. Her body throbbed with desire.

*I'm not dreaming.*

She rolled over, her eyes picking out his outline in the dim moonlight. He was staring at her. Then he leaned in, kissing her slowly, tempting her lips, teasing out her tongue to tangle with his.

"Scott," she breathed, and fit her naked body to his.

"I'm sorry I couldn't get here sooner," he said against her mouth, his hips rocking against hers.

"You're here now." Which she could barely believe.

"You left the window open." He sounded surprised, pleased. Hungry. He reached between them, his fingertips stroking down her stomach before reaching lower. He'd find her wet, she thought. She was slick for him, eager. She parted her thighs as he shuddered.

"I wanted to do this the first time I saw you," he said, and she laughed.

"When I was threatening you with a golf club?"

His chuckle against her skin was like silk, and he leaned lower, kisses circling her aching, sensitive nipples. He drew one into his mouth, swirling around it with his tongue, and she gasped, arching her back involuntarily, filling his mouth with her. Each pulling suck made the wet heat between her legs pulse, and she rubbed her thighs together, whimpering. She felt the bead of wetness at the head of his cock, tracing against her thigh, and she tried to angle him closer to where she really needed him.

He pulled away, breathless. "I wanted you," he repeated, and his eyes looked almost mystical in their intensity, "ever since I saw you in the moonlight."

"Scott," she echoed, and kissed him hard.

He pulled away long enough to grab a foil packet, and she watched as he rolled on the condom with hands that shook. She knew how he felt. It was still unreal— still dreamlike. But at the same time, she couldn't *think*. She could only feel.

And she felt as if she was on fire.

When he covered her body with his, she parted her thighs, almost crying with gratitude when she felt the broad tip of his cock pressing into her. Her hand reached down to guide him. Slowly, he stroked along her passage, dueling with her now erect clit.

She cried out, arching like a bow handle, and he shuddered as he moved lower, pressed deep, her already slick pussy encompassing him.

She gasped at the feeling of his hard, long length

filling her, and for a second, her mind went blank. It had been too long since she'd had sex. Way too long. And she couldn't remember it ever feeling like this.

He moved back, then surged forward, the friction against her clit and G-spot nearly made her scream. She tilted her pelvis up, her knees hooking on his hips as she dragged her nails down his back, crushing her breasts against his chest.

"Amanda," he groaned as he moved into her, with long, slow, gliding strokes that drove her mad.

*More, more, more,* her mind chanted, and she lifted herself to meet each thrust. She urged him forward, shifting, kissing whatever she could reach.

His measured strokes got faster. Their breathing was ragged, urgent.

Soon, they were moving with crazed energy. She could feel it starting in the pit of her stomach, that quivering pleasure that seemed to radiate like an explosion.

Then the orgasm tore through her, and she shrieked in pleasure, clutching around him spasmodically, the amazing sensations propelling her mindlessly forward in unbelievable pleasure.

He shouted in response, and his hips rocked into her, pounding against her...and to her shock, another orgasm blasted, an aftershock of the first, almost as powerful. She bit his shoulder, shuddering against him as he drove against her.

In the quivering aftermath, she felt stunned. As though she might wake up, at any moment. He held her tight, then eased out of her, heading to the bathroom to take care of the condom.

*Now what?*

She was wide-awake, even though she wondered if she was still dreaming.

Would he just leave via the window? Pretend that it *was* just a dream?

She'd never done a fling before. Isn't that what they usually did?

He came back to bed, still naked, climbing in beside her. "I hope you don't mind," he said, his voice husky, "but I'm exhausted."

"It's almost four in the morning," she conceded, thrilled that he wouldn't be leaving. "Of course you're tired."

"Aren't you?" he said, yawning.

She realized immediately that she was. Her limbs started feeling heavy. Now that she was relieved to know what was going on, she felt all the tension seep out of her. She blinked heavily, then smiled in the dark as his arm wound around her waist.

"Consider this an appetizer," he murmured, pressing hot kisses against the back of her neck. "After a few hours of sleep, I'll do that right."

Her smile broadened. "I'll hold you to that." She snuggled against him.

She heard his breathing going slow, heavy, even.

"Scott?" she breathed.

"Hmm?"

She swallowed. "Scott…are you in The Player's Club?"

"Just joined," he muttered.

Her eyes flew open, and her body tensed. So did his, she noticed.

"G'night," he said quickly, releasing her body, then rolling away from her.

She noticed it was a while before either of them went to sleep.


SCOTT WOKE UP DISORIENTED. The sun was slanting over the bed from the wrong angle, shining in his face. The bed was nice, but it wasn't as large as he was used to.

And there was a very soft body next to him.

A very soft, very *naked* body.

*Amanda,* he thought. She was still sleeping, her eyes closed, her cheekbone a wonderful curve to a strong chin, her pale hair in loose tangled waves across her ivory pillow. He leaned down, breathing in her perfume.

His body went hard in a flash.

He ought to wake her up, he thought. Maybe they should talk. About what happened last night. About moving forward. He didn't know if that was something she did on a regular basis—did she even want him there, still? Did she wake up with guys?

He frowned.

As if sensing him, she scooted backward, her curving buttocks nuzzling against his cock. She let out a breathy little sigh and rolled over. Her raspberry tipped breasts jutted upward.

He grimaced. Then he leaned down, pulling another condom out of his pants on the floor. Rolling it on, he stroked her body with his fingertips gently. He tasted her silky skin, pressing tender kisses down her stomach.

Then he moved between her thighs.

She woke up with a jolt, then a low growl of pleasure as his tongue worked her. He felt her clit tighten and tasted the sweet wetness as her body got ready. He stroked her, then kissed her thighs, grazing them with his teeth.

She moaned, arching her back, her head pushed into the pillows as her hips lifted to meet him.

He stretched on top of her, his cock throbbing as he positioned himself at her entrance. Her eyes were sloe-eyed and sexy, her pouty lips curved in a come-here-you smile. He nipped at her neck, sucking hard as his cock slid in. She was tight—wonderfully, mind-bendingly tight, and he moved slow, almost afraid he'd hurt her. She gasped, her legs curling around his, her hips angling up to take even more of him.

"Scott…" she rasped. "You feel…so…*good*…"

He didn't trust his vocal chords to answer. Instead, he withdrew, then flexed, pressing deeper into her. He slowly got into a rocking rhythm, stopping only to lean down, feasting on one breast, then the other.

"Yes," she hissed, then pushed to roll him onto his back. She rolled her hips and his mind went blank with pure pleasure for a shocking moment. He inhaled sharply, then shuddered as his fingers dug into her hips, stilling her.

"How, woman," he panted. "How do you *move* like that?"

Her smile was pure, wicked sex. To demonstrate, she rolled again…one sweet, slow gyration that seemed to put all his sensation right in his cock. He sat up, holding her tight as her legs wrapped around his waist.

He kissed her hard. She bit his lower lip, riding him

in a steady, relentless rhythm, her fingers clawing at his shoulders. He gripped her hips, driving himself upward.

Their movements were less controlled—more intense. She was gasping softly, her breath getting choppy and harsh as her body moved against his. Her thighs clenched around his waist, her nipples like pebbles against his chest.

*"Scott!"* she finally screamed, her head back, her whole body convulsing.

He felt her body milking him, and he couldn't have stopped from coming if a gun were to his temple. His release tore through him savagely, and he groaned loud against her throat, his body jerking upward as she kept clutching him, rubbing her body against his.

It seemed to go on forever. When it did let him go, he collapsed against the bed, her on top of him.

After a long moment, he felt her trembling against him. Alarmed, he looked up.

Her blue eyes danced with merriment. "I guess that'll teach me to leave my window open."

He laughed hoarsely. "Let that be a lesson to you."

"Care to teach me anything else?"

He smiled. "Anything you want," he heard himself say. "As soon as humanly possible."

Her smile was like the sun, blinding him. Chuckling, she rolled off him. He got up to clean himself up.

He didn't know what he was getting himself into. And right now, he really did not care.

Just as long as he got to touch this woman again.

"Um…Scott?"

"Yeah?" he called from the bathroom.

"About last night."

"Yeah," he echoed, smiling to himself. "Last night certainly was something…"

"It was a Player's Club meeting, wasn't it?"

He froze, staring at himself in the mirror.

*You're not supposed to tell* anybody, *remember?*

He ran the water, splashed his face, rinsed his mouth. Then slowly walked out. "Sorry. What?"

She tilted her head, studying him like a curious bird. A curious, tenacious bird. "You said last night that you were a member of The Player's Club."

"The…what club?"

Her eyebrow arched. "Really?" she murmured. "You're going to go that route. *Really.*"

He sighed. He could lie if he had to—it was just that he frankly sucked at it. "I don't want to talk about it."

She took a deep breath. "Listen, I'm not judging you. I'm just… I just wanted to know—"

"I don't know much," he interrupted. "I mean, I don't know really *anything.* I'm not even really in-volved."

She still looked skeptical. "Do you know how to become a member?" she pressed. "Because I want to become one."

He stared back at her, hard. "How did you wind up there?"

She blushed—he could see it spreading over her pale skin, her cheeks, even down her neck and her chest. "I followed you. I pretended I was a dancer."

He gaped. "You faked your way in?" The sheer moxie of the move floored him.

She shrugged delicately. "I've been fascinated with The Player's Club," she admitted.

Suddenly, it all made sense. Her cornering him at the club…inviting him back. Making love to him like some kind of feral sex goddess.

*She's some kind of hell-raiser. Adrenaline junkie.*

And she thought *he* was one, as well.

He sighed heavily. "Listen, I'm not supposed to tell *anyone* about it. Anyone hears that I blabbed, I'm getting kicked out."

"I'm not going to tell a soul," she promised.

He sat down on the bed. "Good." Disconcerted, he started reaching for his clothes. He had to think about this.

Was she using him?

*Does it really matter?*

She tapped his shoulder. "How do you join? Because I want in. I've always been fascinated by it, and…it's just what I need." A determined expression crossed her face. "I mean it. I want *in*."

"I don't know," he said. "I sort of fell into it, myself. But I think people can, um, vouch for people. Bring people in. Although I don't remember seeing any women involved."

She smiled. "I know it's a huge favor, but…would you vouch for me?"

He stopped what he was doing, staring at her over his shoulder. "Is this what all this was about?"

Now, she looked offended. "I have sex because I want to have sex," she said, and her voice trembled with anger. "I wanted to have it with you. If you'll recall, I was the one who approached you, before I even knew you might be in the club."

Her eyes were an incandescent blue, like a welder's torch. "I believe you," he said. "But right now, I'm not even sure I'm in."

"What does that mean?"

"I have to do three challenges," he said, remembering the sleep-deprived haze of the previous night. "In one month. Tough, weird challenges. If I make it, I'm in."

"And if you're in, you could vouch for me?"

"I don't even know that *I* can make it."

"You'll make it." She smiled brightly. "I can help you with that."

He stared at her. "How do you know that?"

"Trust me. I'm resourceful," she said, her face shining with confidence. "Especially when I want something badly. Believe me, I want this more badly than I can remember wanting anything for a long time."

He stared at her.

*Including me?*

She cleared her throat. "So, what are the goals?"

He wracked his fuzzy mind, trying to remember what he'd agreed to. "I need to do a vision quest in the Mojave. Crash an off-the-hook, epic, impossible-to-get-into party. And, er...run."

"Run?" she repeated, frowning.

He rubbed his hands over his face. "With the bulls. In Pamplona." He sighed again. Then he pulled on his pants. "You know, this is a bad idea."

"This sounds perfect," she pressed. "I think—no,

I *know* I can do this. I can help you out, and then you can help me out. We'll help each other!"

He knew that feeling. Which was why he didn't want anyone—even a gorgeous, hell-on-wheels-in-bed blonde—to possibly jeopardize his chance. "Sorry. I just don't think it's going to work."

She frowned. She wasn't pouting—as Kayla might in her place—she wasn't using passive-aggressive techniques, guilting him or seducing him. Although honestly, part of him wouldn't mind it if she tried seducing him to change his mind...

*Knock it off,* he scolded his penis. *Let me do the thinking for once.*

She sighed. "Well, you've got a right to do what you want."

He nodded, feeling a little guilty anyway. "Um... well."

"Well."

She just wanted him because of his connections, he thought, bitterness stabbing at him like a switchblade. He lashed out.

"Guess I'll be staying away from windows, then."

Her eyes widened, and if he didn't know better, he'd swear she looked hurt. She sat up straight like he'd pinched her.

Then her eyes narrowed. She leaned down on the bed next to him, lanky and nude. Her smile was sweet...somehow too sweet.

"Well, with all these adventures, you won't have time to climb through any windows," she mused. "And since I'll have nothing better to do, I guess I'll just hang out with my best friend."

He pulled his shirt over his head, standing up. He made for the door.

Her next words stopped him cold.

"Did I mention my best friend's a reporter?" she asked. "One who'd probably *love* to do a feature about The Player's Club?"

# 5

AMANDA SAT UNCOMFORTABLY cross-legged on the hard-packed sand, wondering absently how in the hell she'd ever considered this a good idea.

*You wanted to be here. You used blackmail to do it.*

A little fact she was still regretting.

"Fine," Scott had said. "You can go with me to the Mojave. And if you make it—if you don't complain or chicken out—then I'll vouch for you. But if you don't, then you can't tell *anyone*. Not your reporter, not anyone."

She'd agreed, and one weekend later, she was here in the Mojave.

She was in this position partially for her desire for adventure, she admitted, but the rest of it was out of pure spite. The thought of him sleeping with her, then saying he wasn't going to anymore because she'd asked about the Club, had struck her as horribly unfair. Maybe he was the adventurous type, maybe he went through women like bottled water.

Whatever, she thought with hostility. She was tired

of being the "nice" girl who was understanding, kind. And boring.

*Well-behaved women rarely make history.*

"Now, we're going to enter the mindset of the vision quest. Please take a deep breath, and listen to the sounds of nature," the dreadlocked guide, Rebecca, said in her best earth-goddess impersonation. There were seventeen other people there with Amanda and Scott. From what Amanda could tell, there were several people who had done this particular camping adventure several times. Their backpacks were well-worn, their hiking boots covered with dust. A few wore tie-dye T-shirts and sported pleasantly vacant smiles, suggesting either a state of camping Zen or perhaps an herbal enhancement. Other people were more like Amanda. Several looked like business types—they had brand-new camp equipment and kept sneaking peeks at their watches. They did not look amused by Rebecca's encouragement.

Amanda tried, she really did. She closed her eyes. The stillness was startling. She heard all the other campers' slight shifts of movement, nervous coughs.

After what seemed like forever, Rebecca sighed. "All right. You've picked your camping spots. Today, I'm sending you out to go three days and nights into the wilderness. Some of you will find wisdom. Some of you may even have visions."

Amanda glanced at the guy to her left, who smiled at her with low-lidded, red-rimmed eyes. *Ten bucks says this guy already had a vision,* Amanda thought, then shook her head.

"Drink your water. Blow your whistle if you run into

any trouble, and remember, you'll be leaving a check-in note with your camp buddy every morning, to ensure that you stay safe all three days. All right? Great! Get to it!"

Scott walked alongside Amanda, not looking directly at her. "Doing okay, camp buddy?"

She nodded. They'd scouted sites together the day before, and she'd tossed and turned her way through the night in her new sleeping bag. "Hanging in there," she said.

He nodded, and they kept walking silently.

*Why couldn't he have gotten a four-star hotel in Bali as an adventure?*

But of course, she didn't have to be here. She'd forced, connived and coerced her way here. There was a big, fat "Be careful what you wish for" proverb here, but she didn't want to think about it.

They reached the canyon that split their two "camp" sites. "I'll leave a note checking in," she said woodenly, starting to strike out toward her solitary plateau.

"My site isn't too far from yours," Scott called to her, stopping her. "So yell if you get into any trouble, okay?"

The fact that he actually said it warmed her. "I won't get into any trouble," she answered him, lacking the confidence to mean it.

She went off to her campsite, watching with concern as he vanished through a canyon not far away. He was camped on top of a small mesa, but one of the conditions of the vision quest was that they couldn't be in eyesight of each other. So once he disappeared, she was completely alone.

She frowned. Okay. Three days and nights. No music. No, er, food. She put down her gallons of water and her backpack, and got to work setting up camp.

After an hour, she'd already cut her thumb on a sharp rock. The tarp she was supposed to be using as a tent had become an unwitting parasail, dragging her across the desert before she could get it under control. Her stomach yowled in protest at all the exertion without food. She wished she'd smuggled in a few energy bars or something. Maybe chocolate.

Her stomach *really* yowled when she thought of chocolate.

By the time the sun started setting, she was sweaty, dirty and miserable. She'd taken the tarp and folded it up like a burrito, weighing it down with rocks, then wiggled inside it with her sleeping bag.

She'd done all this because she needed, desperately, to change. To do something that proved her life was more than what it had been.

*How's that working out for you?*

She fell asleep, sweating, curled up on her sleeping bag, the wind like a hair dryer. She didn't even realize she'd fallen into a dream, especially since it felt so real.

She was standing in her candy shop, the first day she'd opened. Orders were piling in: customers were standing four-deep from the counter. She moved endlessly, rolling truffles, dusting them in cocoa, painting some with gold leaf and decorating them with sugared violets. She was so busy, she never knew if it was day or night.

Then, suddenly, Scott walked in, and everyone else disappeared.

"Come with me," he said, reaching for her, a wicked, sexy grin on his face.

"I can't," she said. "I've got too much work to do."

"It's just work," he said.

"If I don't have this, I don't have anything," she protested.

He was naked, standing in front of her, looking more delectable than all the candy in her shop put together. "Come with me," he repeated.

She shook her head, holding her spatula in a death grip. "I can't."

"Why not?"

*"I'm scared."*

Those two words surprised her so much, she actually dropped her spatula.

The shop drifted away, and it was just the two of them, in her bed, back in her apartment. "What are you scared of?" he whispered to her.

She hesitated. "I've been driven all my life. Everything in my family was about running the restaurant my parents owned. I started working there when I was maybe ten. It was successful. My parents expected nothing less from it, and from my brothers and I. So I learned to be successful." Tears tumbled down her cheeks. "I married my husband because he was a chef, and I thought we had so much in common. We owned the shop together. But he didn't love me...not passionately or anything. And I didn't really love him."

"So what do you want now?"

She took a deep breath, turning and burying her head against his chest. "I want someone to love me passionately," she said. "I want to stop worrying about whether or not I'm successful. I want to live life, not just sprint through it."

"You can have that," he murmured. "All that, and more."

"But business is all I'm good at!" she wailed. "I don't know how to do anything else. I keep thinking I'm screwing this up."

He chuckled. "Screwing *what* up?"

"This. You, me. Us." She winced. "Not that I'm angling for a relationship. I don't even know if I could handle one. But..." She took a deep breath. "I've never felt anything like I feel when I'm with you."

"What's wrong with that?"

"I'm tired of trying to be something I'm not to impress you," she said, realizing as the words came out that it was true. "I want you to like me for who I am."

"Then be who you are."

She shook her head.

"Come to me," he breathed. "Come to me, just as you are. And see."

She opened her eyes. It was still pitch-black out, but the moon was full, and she was momentarily dazzled by the brilliant field of stars stretching out across the sky. She'd never seen so many stars in her life. In cities, you *couldn't* see stars like this.

*Come to me.*

It'd felt so real.

It was probably foolish, but the moon was so incredibly bright, it was like walking through a negative of the landscape. She could see where she was going. And she found herself tramping through the brush, through the ravine, up the slope. Until she got to the mesa.

Until she got to Scott.

He did have a tarp set up like a tent, and his sleeping bag was bundled up. She wondered if she would wake him.

"Who's there?" she heard him say, his voice deep and imposing.

She took a breath. "It's me. Amanda."

"Amanda?" he sounded shocked, and he clambered out of the bag clumsily. "Honey, are you all right?"

She started to say yes, but it came out, "No."

He rushed to her side, checking her, his eyes full of concern. "Are you hurt? Do you need the whistle?"

"No," she said, brushing away tears. "It's just…"

He stroked her cheek. "What?"

"I just had to tell you I'm sorry," she admitted through clenched teeth. "It was wrong of me to black-mail you. It's…it's *not* me."

He stared at her, silent.

"I was just so… I just wanted this adventure," she said. "But it's not worth it."

Maybe it was a trick of the light, but he seemed to be smiling. "Thanks for that."

"Okay." Feeling like an idiot, she started to turn, to leave.

"Anything else?" he asked softly.

She let out a choppy laugh.

"And I hate frickin' camping," she bit out. "I'm starving, I couldn't get my tarp up, the ground's really hard, and I'd kill to be in a hotel."

He burst out laughing, a clear, ringing sound that echoed through the night sky.

"Aww, honey," he said, bundling her into his arms

for a hug. She hugged back, hard. Then he leaned down and kissed her. She kissed him, hard and long.

Then she pulled away, gasping, staring at him.

"What?"

*"You taste like chocolate!"*

He looked guilty, then sly. "I could share."

"You'd better!"

He led her to his sleeping bag, next to his backpack. "What'll I get in exchange?" he said. "Out here, chocolate's as precious as gold."

She smiled back. "What do you want?"

He opened the sleeping bag. "It's an extra-wide."

It would still be snug, she realized. Too hot. Then she saw the heat in his eyes and realized that perhaps that wouldn't be a problem.

"Only if you're sure," she demurred, but felt her lips curving into a smirk.

"It's for survival," he said with mock solemnity, and she giggled.

"I'm trading my virtue for a chocolate bar," she muttered, unable to keep the smile out of her voice.

"Bar, nothing." He produced a gold-foil-wrapped truffle. "San Francisco's finest."

She read the label on the foil.

*CandyLove.*

It was one of hers. That is, it was from her shop.

And it was her favorite.

She stared for a long moment, and he cleared his throat.

"You okay?"

"Holy crap," she murmured, holding the truffle. "I've had a vision."

*WELL, THINGS ARE DEFINITELY looking up.*

Scott had been lying on top of his sleeping bag, sweating his ass off, wondering what in the world he'd been thinking when he decided that he wanted to do this before he died. Somehow, the thought of a vision quest sounded more mystical and life-changing when he'd thought about it in the abstract, or saw movies about Native Americans who did it.

So far, it was just sleeping on a rock and subsisting only on chocolate he'd packed on a whim.

Then he'd heard noises. What the hell lived out in the desert, anyway? Burros, he was pretty sure, but that wasn't really loud enough to be a burro. So what, then? Some kind of wildcat?

*If this is bad, what the heck are the bulls going to be like?*

Then Amanda had trudged up, looking hot and cute and grim at the same time. Her white-blond hair was pulled up in a high ponytail and she had a smudge of dirt on her high cheekbone. She looked like a cross between a Valkyrie and an Indian princess.

He suddenly wanted nothing more than to touch her. Especially after her confession and apology. She actually seemed to believe that he loved "roughing it," that this barren, burning piece of earth was a slice of heaven for him.

Of course, she was now snuggled in his sleeping bag, so he wasn't going to argue with her.

She sighed as she slowly chewed the chocolate he'd given her, her eyes closed. She looked dreamy, a smile blooming on her face. "God, this is marvelous," she said, nuzzling against his chest. "You are a lifesaver."

"Cooling off?"

She stretched out on top of the bag. "Getting better."

He cleared his throat. "You know, the best way to cool down is to expose as much of your body as possible, I think."

She opened one eye, peering at him with amused skepticism. "That so?"

"Scout's honor." He crossed his chest with his fingers.

"Obviously I was never a Scout," she joked, her smile turning mischievous. "I guess I'd better take your word for it."

He leaned down and kissed her, tasting the rich ribbons of chocolate from the truffle she'd eaten. She used her tongue to tickle his. His cock went from semihard to rigid in a rush.

He'd slept in shorts, just in case. It took less than a second to strip them off. He focused on helping her out of her shorts and tank top.

When they did, they were breathless from laughing. The minute her warm naked skin touched his, all his laughter vanished, leaving only breathlessness.

She responded as he pressed hot kisses just behind her earlobe, then nibbled the sensitive flesh. She pressed her whole body against him, and he could feel the hard pebbles of her nipples against his chest as the curls at the juncture of her thighs nestled his cock. He shuddered, struggling to keep a grip. He nipped at her neck, licking the well of her collarbone, kissing the hollow of her throat. She wound her fingers in his hair, keeping him flush against her, and hooked one leg over his hip.

The two of them strained against the confines of the sleeping bag. He took one of her breasts in his mouth as he held her hip, his cock tracing her stomach. She cried out softly, arching her back, rubbing her hips against him. He suckled gently, deliberately, when it was all he could do not to lay her back and plunge inside her.

"Scott, did you bring a condom?" she whispered.

It took him a second to get his bearings. Then he rummaged around his clothes, pulling out the condoms he'd optimistically kept in his jacket pocket. "Be prepared," he murmured with a lightning grin.

"I'm so glad you were a Scout," she purred as he hastily rolled it on. She reached for him, offering him her other breast and shifting slightly so she was under him. He was between her legs, tracing the areola of one breast with his tongue as he caressed the other with his palm. She trembled beneath him, her hands clawing gently at his shoulders, her legs going as wide as the bag would allow.

He'd thought the desert was hot. Suddenly, the world was on fire. He didn't notice the discomfort of his surroundings, or the hardness of the ground. All that mattered was the woman beneath him. It was heaven.

He moved back to her mouth, feasting on her full lips. She rubbed restlessly against his cock, making soft, insistent sounds in the back of her throat. The sounds were like throwing gasoline on a fire. He reached between them, his fingers probing the fissure to her sex. She was already damp—already *wet,* and his cock throbbed painfully. Still, he took the time to circle the erect nubbin of flesh nestled between her folds.

She cried out again, her hips bucking against his hand. "Oh, *yes,*" she said, her eyes alight. "I just want you inside me."

He positioned himself, then slid into her slowly, groaning at how tight she felt around him. She sighed, shuddering, and he could feel her pussy rippling around his shaft.

He propped himself up on his elbows, moving his hips against her, then withdrawing by slow inches. It was brutal to be patient, but the effect was worth it. They moved gracefully, her hips lifting to meet his every deliberate thrust. Her hair was against his pillow in a white-gold cloud, her eyes were closed, her mouth open in a silent gasp of delight.

"Amanda," he breathed, unable to put what he was feeling into any other words. He'd never had sex like this. Not with anyone else, not ever.

She mewled, wrapping her legs around his waist.

He lost it. Slow and deliberate made way for hot, hard and fast. His hips flexed and pumped, and each time he buried himself fully inside her, they both groaned, growing increasingly louder. She clawed at his back, and he bucked against her, the two of them moving like mating animals as the need grew and built on itself.

He had to wait. Everything in his body was screaming at him to come, but he needed to make sure that she was satisfied. Then, he could...

*"Ohh!"* She tilted her head back, and he could feel her pussy contracting against him, hard as a fist, stroking his cock with a rippling strength that surprised him. Before he could help himself, his orgasm blazed

through him, and he shuddered against her, his hips jerking as he spilled himself inside her.

When it was over, he nearly blacked out, overwhelmed by the sensation.

He rolled to his side...or at least, as best he could, since they were still sausage-cased in the sleeping bag. "Wow." It was all he could manage to say.

She made incoherent happy sounds for several long moments, nuzzling against him, before he left her to take care of the condom. "I could get to like camping," she eventually said in a sleepy voice.

He laughed. "You've hit it, now you're going to sleep on me?" he said, with a small yawn.

"There's always the morning," she said, snuggling up against him. Then her eyes widened. "Unless... Did you want me to go back to my, er, bag? You know, my campsite?"

"Why would I want that?" he said, holding her tighter.

*Because this isn't a relationship, you dweeb.* He suddenly winced, realizing he wasn't really acting as if this was an affair. He was acting as if she were a girlfriend.

"Did you want to go back?"

She shook her head, looking puzzled.

"If you go back, there's no telling what might happen to you," he said. "If you stay here, we can, you know, watch each other's back."

A slow smile crept over her face. "So we're just being practical."

"Exactly."

She kissed his throat, his shoulder. Stroked his chest, causing him to tremble slightly.

"I guess I could stay for one more night," she said slowly.

He smiled. He'd never been good at hit-it-and-quit-it; he wasn't a screw-around guy. But if she was, then he'd take what he could get.

He'd just have to deal with it one day—and more important, one *night*—at a time.

# 6

"NOW CAN YOU TELL ME what in the hell possessed you to traipse out to the middle of nowhere with a bunch of wannabe hippies on some *vision quest?*" Jackie asked without preamble as she met Amanda at the lobby doors of her newspaper's headquarters.

"It seemed like a good idea at the time. Ready for our Wednesday lunch?"

Jackie rolled her eyes. "I know you want to get all adventure-ish and explorer-y and whatnot, but really. That's not an adventure. That's torture. And not the fun kind."

"I think I figured that out on my own," Amanda said.

As they walked, Jackie continued to stare at her. "Right. What's really going on?"

They arrived at Fat Slice pizza, each getting a slice of fat, gooey, calorie-laden excess with the ironic large diet soda. "What do you mean?" Amanda asked, in her best innocent tone of voice.

"You're lying. Or at least fibbing," Jackie said, poking Amanda in the shoulder as they walked down the sidewalk toward the Square. "You're keeping a secret."

Amanda had trouble swallowing her bite of pizza—guilt felt like a lump in her throat. "Um…"

Jackie's eyes went wide. "You *got* some!"

Amanda frowned. "Thanks. I was thinking about putting it on a billboard, but now I won't need to."

"Who? Who?" They sat down on the low wall along the Square, and Jackie's gaze shone on her like an interrogator's light. "It wasn't… Was it the neighbor? Fire-escape guy?"

Amanda felt the blush crawl up, and Jackie whooped before she could confirm it. She hated keeping any secret from Jackie, but she'd promised: it wasn't her secret to tell. In the meantime, she'd never promised to keep her sex life a secret.

*Lesser of two evils,* she rationalized.

"So how was it?" Jackie asked with gusto. "Come on. Spare no detail."

Amanda spared a lot of details, like the club, and her dancing, et cetera. But she said that they'd met up one night in a dark hallway, and then she'd invited him into her window…

"And the rest was history," Amanda said with a slow grin.

"So *he's* why you went camping," Jackie said. "Well, I'm not for roughing it, but to each her own. What's going to be your next move?"

"Not sure," Amanda hedged, getting to eat some of her now-cold pizza. "I'm sort of playing it by ear."

Jackie went silent, studying her. Amanda sighed, sensing trouble coming.

"You know, you don't have to have all your adventures with one guy," Jackie said. "There are plenty of bad boys in the sea."

"Yeah, I know," Amanda said. "I'm happy with the one I've got, thanks."

"Uh-oh. You're getting attached."

Amanda scrunched up her face. "You make it sound like I named a stray puppy."

"Didn't you? You are *so* fling challenged," Jackie whined. "A total serial monogamist."

"And that's a *bad* thing," Amanda observed.

"This time it is." Jackie wiped her mouth and hands with a napkin. "Repeat after me. I am only interested in casual sex."

Amanda's blush burned across her cheeks again. "Out loud? Seriously?"

"I am only interested in casual sex," Jackie repeated with menace.

"This is like that time you tried to get me to say 'penis' in a movie theater," Amanda grumbled. "I'm not a prude, Jackie, I just—"

*"I am only interested..."* Jackie shouted. Amanda quickly shushed her.

"Okay! I am only interested in casual sex! I have no interest in pursuing anything more, with anyone, much less Scott sex-in-a-sleeping-bag Ferrell! All right?"

Jackie smirked. "Tell me you won't see him again, then."

Amanda crossed her arms. "No."

"So you *are* getting serious about him." Jackie shook her head. "This is the first guy you've seen since your divorce, Amanda. I'm not trying to get all in your business..."

"Sure you are," Amanda said, without venom.

"Well, okay, yeah I am. But only because I'm worried about you." And to her credit, Jackie really did look concerned.

Amanda sighed. "I'm still going to see him—and yeah, sleep with him—but it's not exactly what you think."

Jackie's ears perked up, and Amanda bit her tongue. "You're keeping another secret."

"For now," Amanda said. "It's not that big a deal."

Jackie might be writing an advice column, but she was too much the reporter *not* to smell blood in the water. "Can I ask questions? Could you maybe mime it?"

"No questions, no miming," Amanda insisted, with a little laugh. Her cell phone rang. "Sorry," she told Jackie. She didn't recognize the number and wondered absently if it was Scott.

"Hello, is this Amanda?" A woman's voice asked.

"Yes...this is Amanda." *Who is this?*

"Oh, good," the woman said. "This is Tina."

"Tina..."

"From the Bettie Pages. The burlesque dance troupe."

"Oh!" Amanda said, taking a step away from Jackie. "Right, right. How are you?"

"Shorthanded," Tina said, with a desperate laugh. "Is there any way you could step in for me? I've got a huge gig coming up this weekend—you wouldn't believe how high profile—and three of my dancers are down with the flu."

"Dancing…" Amanda said, squirming slightly. That had been a ruse—a way to get in, find out more about the club. She looked at Jackie, who was listening intently. "Um…"

"I'll wash your car. I'll babysit your firstborn. I'm really in a jam here."

Amanda thought about it. It *had* been fun—but the next day, it had seemed like a dream. Now the mere thought of it made her stomach knot unpleasantly. "Er, I think my dancing career is over."

"I had to try," Tina said, sighing. "If you reconsider it, will you at least give me a call?"

"All right," Amanda promised, then signed off.

"Dancing career?" Jackie said, eyebrow raised.

"Long story."

"I've got an hour for lunch."

Amanda smiled. "It's sort of part of the secret."

"It's not, like, a *dangerous* secret, right?" Jackie asked suddenly. "I mean, this guy's not signing you up in some cult or something?"

Amanda shook her head, but her laugh sounded a little breathless—a little guilty, to her own ears. "Not a cult," she said. *More like a club.*

"All right." Jackie sounded unconvinced. "Do you think it's worth it?"

Amanda contemplated the crust of her pizza. She'd danced nearly topless, spent almost a week out in the Mojave, and was having bed-breaking sex with her neighbor…whom she was blackmailing in order to get into The Player's Club.

*At least I'm not boring, right?*

"Is it worth it?" she echoed. "I sure hope so."

THIS TIME, THE CLUB MEETING didn't take place at the warehouse or the basement across the street. It was in the back room of a sports bar, someplace loud and rowdy. It was only one in the morning—the bar was still going strong, meaning the crew was packed like sardines in the small location, fighting the noise of the crowds and the TVs.

George was doing beer funnels, and Lincoln looked unamused.

"Anything to report?" Lincoln asked, and Scott strained to hear him over the sounds of drunken cheering from the other side of the wall.

"I did the first challenge," Scott said, forcing himself to be louder. "Now what?"

Finn hooted, giving him a thumbs-up, and the rest of the room made various noises of approval.

Lincoln nodded. "Now, on to your second challenge—"

"Wait a minute," George interrupted, sneering at Scott. "Do we have proof that you went out there, camping, in the desert?"

Scott looked at Finn, who shrugged. Lincoln's jaw clenched.

"I've got some pictures," Scott replied. *And I've got a girl who can verify exactly where I was.*

Scott grinned at that thought. Apparently, George took the grin as a challenge.

"Had fun, huh?" George sounded distinctly derisive. "Jeez. Frickin' nerd challenge…"

Finn held up his hands. "Hey, you know the rules of the Club, cuz," he said quickly, cutting off any more of George's diatribe. "We've always run it this way. Since the beginning."

"When it was just Finn, Tucker, a few other guys… and me," Lincoln added.

The fury and hatred in George's eyes was quickly veiled…so quickly, Scott wondered if maybe he'd imagined it. George's expression was now one of reluctant acceptance.

"So the guy went camping. Big deal," George scoffed.

"The first of three big deals," Lincoln segued gracefully. "Which means he's on to the second challenge."

"I'd like some clarification on that, actually," Scott said. "I wasn't really that clear on what a 'huge party' entailed, so I—"

"Oh, no," George spoke up, stepping forward. "You're not weaseling out of this one."

"Just crash a party," Lincoln said, crossing his arms. "You need to get ready for those bulls."

"He didn't say he'd crash just any party," George protested. "He wanted to crash something epic."

"Whatever."

George's eyes flashed with contempt, and he took a step toward Lincoln. Lincoln appeared casual, but Scott could tell his fists were balled, knuckles white.

George outweighed Lincoln by a good forty pounds or so, but it looked like fat. Scott would put money on Lincoln any day.

Finn quickly stepped in. "Cut it out, guys. Focus."

Lincoln didn't back down. Neither did George.

Finn looked at the ceiling. "George has a point. It has to be a *challenge,* Linc. If it's easy—if it's something he could do without breaking a sweat—what's the point?"

Lincoln said nothing.

"Remember?" Finn said, and Scott could only hear him because he was standing so close. "When we started this. If it didn't scare the crap out of us, why do it?"

Lincoln sighed heavily. Then, slowly, he took a step back.

"What did you have in mind, George?"

George preened. "There is this huge, off-the-chain party happening downtown in about a week. It's been sold out for months, and only A-listers are allowed."

"I suppose you're going," Lincoln said. He sounded bored.

"Hell, yeah," George said, too intent on bragging to get Lincoln's tone. "I paid ten large to get in."

Tucker choked out a cough. "You paid ten thousand dollars to go to a *party?* What, does that come with a car?"

George ignored him. He looked at Scott.

"You crash *that,*" he said, with a note of challenge, "and you'll have pulled off something. They've got bouncers that are ex-marines. Every invitation has a QR code that can't be replicated—"

Tucker tsked.

"And you've got to be on the list. Anybody taking pictures is going to be thrown out. It's for this insane magazine, completely depraved."

Scott swallowed. "So I just need to get in, right?"

"No, you need to crash it, which means you need to hang out there. Just getting your ass kicked by the bouncer doesn't count."

Scott checked with Lincoln. "Is that the challenge, then?"

Lincoln looked pissed. "Let's put it at fifteen minutes," he said.

"Thirty," George countered.

Finn sighed again. "Split the difference at twenty-two and a half," he said. "Now can we start talking Pamplona?"

After talking logistics—places they could stay, who was going to run with Scott, stuff of that nature—George got bored. He and his crew of five or so guys wandered out to join the last of the bar crowd before they closed the place down. As soon as the door shut behind him, Lincoln went straight to Finn.

"He's getting worse," he said.

Finn didn't have to answer. Scott looked at the others.

"We've got to get rid of him," Tucker announced, and Finn looked insulted.

"Hey. He's my cousin."

"He's an ass," Tucker said, and Scott saw Lincoln hide a lightning grin.

Finn crossed his arms. "The Club started because we wanted to hang out with people who wanted to change their lives. George was in early, near the beginning."

Lincoln rubbed a hand over the back of his neck. Then at Scott, he said, "So. How are you going to get into this party? What can we do to help?"

"I can get you a QR code without blinking," Tucker said.

"Really?"

Tucker smirked. "If I can break into Microsoft, I can get you a stupid party invitation."

"If we help Scott too much," Lincoln pointed out, "George is going to call foul. He's already trying to edge Scott out."

Finn had a troubled expression on his face.

"He knows Scott's more like us," Lincoln continued, "than like him. He wants to make this a big fraternity."

"I know."

"One day, it's going to come down to a vote," Lincoln stated. "And you know he's already got five other guys to back him up. Just at a start."

Finn grimaced. "Let me talk to him, okay?"

Finn left and Scott turned to Lincoln. "That reminds me. Can I invite, er, someone? To become a Player?"

Lincoln's gaze was like a scalpel. "Did you tell anyone?"

"No! No," Scott said quickly, thinking, *She found out on her own.* Technically, he wasn't lying. "But I'd like to bring someone in."

"You have to be a full Player," Tucker said. "Which means you've got to complete your challenges."

"Right," Scott said. "So...you can hook me up with the QR code? With a fake invitation?"

"I can get you past security," Tucker said.

"Too late for that," Finn said, jogging up to them. "George figured that we'd try to help that way. So he's making sure all the bouncers have your picture."

"Damn it," Lincoln growled.

"He's just trying to keep it an honest challenge." But even Finn didn't sound as if he believed it.

"He's trying to keep it an exclusive boys' club that he gets to parade around as vice president of," Lincoln shot back. "When we started this, we were in it to live, remember? Face down things we were too cowardly to do before..."

He paused, glancing at Scott.

"Well, before the Club," he finished, causing Scott to wonder what *before* really meant. What had happened to prompt them to start the Club?

"If someone else helps with the challenges, that's fine," Lincoln continued. "This isn't about proving you've got balls. It's about admitting whether or not you really want to change your life!"

"I *know* that," Finn said, surprisingly serious. "You think I don't?"

The group dissolved into discussion, and Scott tuned out as reality set in.

He now had to crash some stupid, ten-grand-a-ticket party.

And he had absolutely no idea how he was going to do it.

# 7

SCOTT CLIMBED UP the fire escape to Amanda's window. Sure, he could go through the door now—they knew each other, they were dating, stuff like that—but it was two in the morning. Besides, there was a certain sexy danger to it. He was pretty sure she liked the idea of him sneaking in like a burglar, sliding into bed with her.

*She gets turned on because she thinks I'm some dangerous bad boy.*

He gritted his teeth. He liked that, ordinarily. But tonight, he was tired, frustrated. Pissed. And he was fairly certain he was going to get booted from the Club.

*How long is Amanda going to like you then?*

He put it from his mind as he headed for Amanda's bedroom.

She had her light on, a pair of glasses perched on her perky nose, her body swamped in a gray T-shirt that read Alcatraz Triathalon: Dig, Dive, Swim on it. Her hair was pulled back in a ponytail. She was frowning, turning a page.

She looked like a very sexy librarian. He felt his tired body wake up, and he grinned.

"God, you look hot."

She startled, dropping her book. "Oh! What time is it?" She glanced over at her alarm clock, then quickly took off her glasses. "Crap. I was… I mean…"

"I think I'm seeing a whole new side of you, Amanda," he said, taking off his clothes and climbing next to her as she quickly released her hair from its band and pulled off her T-shirt.

"I meant to be more, you know, *ready* for you," she said, huffy.

"What are you reading?" He picked it up, glanced at the cover. "The new *Dresden Files,*" he said appreciatively.

"Just killing time." She quickly turned off the light, but not before he noticed a blush on her cheeks.

He kissed her shoulder, then kissed her neck. "You know, you're sexier in a T-shirt and glasses than most women are in lingerie."

She chuckled softly, then hugged him, hard. Suddenly, he felt twenty feet tall. She curled against him, kissing him, gently at first, then a bit more intently.

He sighed, holding her to him.

"You seem different tonight," she said. "Something wrong?"

He grimaced. He should've hid that better. "Just a little speed bump."

"The Club?" She leaned up. "What's going on?"

"Nothing," he said, trying to caress her back to her nestled place in his arm. "Just some challenge issues, that's all."

"The party?"

He shouldn't have told her, he realized. The woman was like a terrier. "Yeah."

"What's the problem?"

"Do we really need to talk about it now?" he answered, trying to sound persuasive—but, to his own ears, sounding a little grumpy.

*Smooth, real smooth.*

She turned the light back on, then spun on him. "Don't do that."

"Do what?"

"Do the 'don't worry, sunshine, let Sugar Daddy take care of business' thing," she shot back, crossing her arms. "It drives me absolutely *nuts*. My ex-husband used to do that all the time."

She had an ex-husband? "Which would explain why he's an ex, I guess," he quipped, trying to roll with it.

"One thing of many, and let's not change the subject." She looked more sympathetic, and leaned her face on one hand, listening intently. "What's going on?"

He sighed. Then he leaned back.

"They picked this party for me. Specifically, this jerk named George picked the party for me," Scott explained. "I need to get into this huge, epic, ten-thousand-dollar-a-ticket party."

She let out a low whistle. "Yikes."

"Tell me about it." He rubbed his eyes with the heels of his palms.

"Any ideas?"

She sounded so confident. As if she had no doubt whatsoever that he'd pull it off. *That makes one of us.*

"I'm still kicking things around," he said. "I figure

I could try to be a busboy, or something. I don't know, maybe blend in with catering. I'm pretty sure I won't pass as a bouncer. And I really, *really* don't want to get arrested for breaking and entering to something like this."

"Wow," she said, and rested her head against his chest. Her hair felt like cool silk on his skin, and she smelled like jasmine and vanilla. The smell calmed him. "And if that doesn't work?"

"Then I guess I'm not going to get in the Club." The sentence caused him a pang.

"Well, that's crap," she said, and he grimaced at her, annoyed. "You're not going to just give up, are you? You're not that kind of man."

He thought about it.

*I've been living in the shadows of these big-ego, big adventure jerk-offs for all my life. I'm tired of being the nice guy that people tell their cool stories to. I want to be the guy that has the stories to tell.*

"I don't want to give up," he said. "I'm not going to give up."

Her expression was filled with approval—and admiration.

That was what he wanted. He wanted to be the guy that put that look on her face.

"What's the party, anyway?"

"Some damned thing…what was it?" He closed his eyes. "Oh, right. The Debauchanalia."

"The Debauch…" She said, then started laughing. "Small world."

"You know it?"

"Strangely enough, yes. And I think I know a way to get you in."

He sat up abruptly, and she squealed in protest as he almost knocked her off the bed. "Seriously?"

"Yes." Her eyes twinkled. "Although, I have to warn you—you might not like how."

"Whatever, I'll take it," he said, excited.

"Perfect." She kissed him, slowly, and moved over him, covering his body with hers.

As he started the delicious slide toward oblivion, he heard her ask the question, "How are you at dancing?"

AMANDA WAS STILL GRINNING as they headed to the party.

"I'm not comfortable with this," Scott muttered.

"Do you know of another way to get into this party?" Amanda replied, trying hard not to laugh. "Listen, this is perfect."

"Yeah, but what if I have to…you know," he said. Then he shook his hips spastically.

She giggled. "What? Have a seizure?"

"Now I *know* I'm not comfortable with this," he said, turning and starting to walk away. She grabbed his arm.

"Sorry, sorry. But don't worry. This is just to get you in," she reassured him.

"Because I can't…no. I *don't* dance."

She could see that, obviously. But he went with her to the side door anyway.

A bruising bouncer that looked like an ex-marine was working, earpiece in, sunglasses on despite the fact that it was nine o'clock. "Who are you?" he snarled.

Amanda felt her heart beating double-time, and

wished once again that she were better at lying. "We're dancers," she said. "We're with the Bettie Pages."

The bouncer glared at Scott. Or at least, he seemed to glare. It was hard to tell with the sunglasses. "He don't look like a dancer."

"We have an act together," Amanda said, trying to bat her eyes without being too ridiculous. She was wearing a tank top and sweats, so it'd be easier to change into her costume. She shot him her most innocent-looking smile.

The bouncer still scowled at them. "I have to call it in."

She felt her palms sweat, and leaned back against Scott. The guy was listening intently to his earpiece.

Suddenly, Tina ran out to the door. "Amanda! Thank God. If you hadn't shown up, I wasn't going to get paid. Where's your friend?"

"He's right here." Amanda gestured to Scott.

Tina was clearly surprised, but she shrugged. "Right now, I'd take you if you were a trained chimp. No offense," she said quickly. She seemed to be running on adrenaline and nerves. "Rinaldo, they're with me, and they're late. I need them in costume and on stage in like ten."

"Right, Tina," the bouncer said with something like an adoring smile. Apparently, the bouncer had a crush on Miss Tina.

"I can't believe that worked," Scott whispered in her ear.

Tina turned to them. "All right. Amanda, you know about the wigs and outfits…but I really wasn't expecting a guy. What does he do?"

What does he do? Amanda blanked…and suddenly felt badly. After all, this was Tina's livelihood. She couldn't exactly leave her high and dry. "Um, are we in a cage, or on a stage?"

"Stage. Good thing, with this crew," Tina said. "They are a hell of a lot more famous, and more rowdy, than the last guys you danced for. I'd be careful when you're crossing the floor."

"I'll make sure nobody touches her." Scott's voice was rich with menace. Tina nodded with approval, even as Amanda shot him a look of surprise.

"Do we have a chair?" Amanda asked.

"I'm sure I can get one. Why?"

"That's the act. I'm sort of doing a…er, lap dance. For him," she improvised.

Tina's eyebrows jumped up.

"Very tasteful, though," Amanda quickly added.

Tina sighed. "I swear, from now on, no more big venues. I don't care how much money they pay. They don't know how to treat artists. I'll go get that chair."

"A lap dance?" Scott exclaimed, then goggled as she stripped down to her underwear in the room Tina had led them to.

"It was all I could think of. She's being nice enough to let you in here. The least you can do is sit on a stage and get entertained," Amanda explained, hastily sliding the hangers on the rod. "What do you think?" She held up a black bra-and-tap-pants number, and another in leopard print.

Amanda watched as Scott swallowed. "The, er, black one."

"Got it." She took off her bra, switching it for the black. "Take off your shirt."

His smile was hungry. He took his shirt off, reaching for her.

"No, not yet," she said with a laugh. "That's going to be your costume."

"What?" He looked down at his chest. He was well-defined...and yummy, she thought, although she'd bet he didn't see it. "Are you sure?" he asked.

"It'll work like gangbusters."

"All right. There's a chair on the stage," Tina said, wild-eyed. "I need you on stage now. I'll have a few more girls coming in after all, but I can't afford an empty stage for long. Can you perform for at least five minutes until I can get the backup dancers on?"

Amanda gritted her teeth, then nodded. "Sure we can. Right, Scott?"

"Right," he said slowly.

"Then let's go."

Amanda held Scott's hand as they wove through the drunken revelry. There were people in various states of undress, dancing, drinking and doing God knows what else. She bet a paparazzo would have a field day if he could get a camera in here.

"They're mostly smashed," she told Scott, as Tina led them onto the smallish wooden stage. "Nobody's going to be paying attention to us."

"I hope not," Scott said, looking pale.

The music kicked up, and Tina grabbed a mike. "And now, presenting...the Bettie Pages!"

Amanda felt her stomach roll as a spotlight hit them,

and a crowd of several hundred suddenly looked at her and the seated Scott.

Tina had apparently taken her literally. The song blasting from the high-tech sound system was "Lap Dance" by Pharrell. It had a driving, insane beat, which helped. She did a few dance steps, some of the burlesque wiggles she'd managed to pick up from her last outing with the Bettie Pages.

The crowd looked bored.

Tina looked like she was going to be sick. Possibly have a heart attack.

And Scott was sweating.

*Scott.* Just being able to focus on him helped Amanda feel better. She moved closer to him, leaning enough to have her cleavage about eye level, and she did a quick bend and snap. He smiled, a sexy, seductive smile.

The heat in her stomach went from nerves to desire in a second, and she reveled gratefully in the change of energy. She scooted closer, her hips swiveling, moving to tease, to caress. She backed up against him, felt his fingers almost touching her…and she danced out of reach.

Pretty soon, she was sure he was sweating for an entirely different reason. She momentarily forgot all about the audience as she danced, teased, caressed and tempted. He reached for her, kissing her neck, his fingers digging into her hips when she straddled his lap.

He held her tight, pressing a hard kiss on her, and she gasped against his mouth. She leaned back, letting him kiss her chin, her throat, between her breasts as her legs wrapped around his waist. It was less a dance, more like a mating ritual. She gyrated with him. He kissed and stroked anything he could get a grip on. She thought she was losing her mind.

She barely made out a low roar of approval as Scott clutched her to him. She got up, dizzy, almost drunk with it. He got up out of the chair, following her.

She didn't know how long they were out there, but suddenly, they were surrounded by other women dancers, in the trademark Bettie Page costumes. Tina gently ushered them off stage.

"Whew!" she said, fanning her face with her fingers. "You two were *hot*."

Amanda felt a blush—and a heat, as her legs throbbed.

Tina handed her clothes to her. "I got a couple of pictures of you. I'll email them tonight," she added, with a wink. "Otherwise, you two have fun. I think we're good now. I've managed to pull together the full crew."

Scott didn't say anything, just grabbed her hand as soon as she'd changed clothes and took her from the building. "I don't know if I can make it to the car," he rasped as they rushed down the street. She almost stumbled and he swung her up over his shoulder.

"Oh, my God," she laughed breathlessly. "You're insane!"

"You," he said, smacking her softly on the ass, "have no idea."

They made it to the car and sped away. She was practically writhing with the heat her body was generating. She wanted sex. She wanted Scott. And she wanted it *now*.

"Traffic jam," he cursed. "Some kind of accident."

# FREE Merchandise is 'in the Cards' for you!

Dear Reader,

### We're giving away FREE MERCHANDISE!

Seriously, we'd like to reward you for reading this novel by giving you **FREE MERCHANDISE** worth over $20. And no purchase is necessary!

You see the Jack of Hearts sticker above? Paste that sticker in the box on the Free Merchandise Voucher inside. Return the Voucher promptly...and we'll send you valuable Free Merchandise!

Thanks again for reading one of our novels—and enjoy your Free Merchandise with our compliments!

*Pam Powers*

Pam Powers

P.S. Look inside to see what Free Merchandise is **"in the cards"** for you!

**W**e'd like to send you two free books to introduce you to the Harlequin® Blaze® series. These books are worth over $10, but they are yours to keep absolutely FREE! We'll even send you 2 wonderful surprise gifts. You can't lose!

**REMEMBER:** Your Free Merchandise, consisting of **2 Free Books** and **2 Free Gifts**, is worth over $20.00! No purchase is necessary, so please send for your Free Merchandise today.

**YOUR FREE MERCHANDISE INCLUDES...**

2 FREE Harlequin® Blaze® Books

**AND** 2 FREE Mystery Gifts

# FREE MERCHANDISE VOUCHER

2 FREE
BOOKS
and
2 FREE
GIFTS

Please send my Free Merchandise, consisting of
**2 Free Books** and **2 Free Mystery Gifts**.
I understand that I am under no obligation to buy
anything, as explained on the back of this card.

### 151/351 HDL FMLT

*Please Print*

FIRST NAME

LAST NAME

ADDRESS

APT.#              CITY

STATE/PROV.       ZIP/POSTAL CODE

## *NO PURCHASE NECESSARY!*

► Detach card and mail today. No stamp needed. ►

© 2011 HARLEQUIN ENTERPRISES LIMITED. ® and ™ are trademarks owned and used by the trademark owner and/or its licensee. Printed in the U.S.A.

H-B-01/12

**The Reader Service - Here's how it works:**

Accepting your 2 free books and 2 free mystery gifts (gifts valued at approximately $10.00) places you under no obligation to buy anything. You may keep the books and gifts and return the shipping statement marked "cancel." If you do not cancel, about a month later we'll send you 6 additional books and bill you just $4.49 each in the U.S. or $4.96 each in Canada. That's a savings of at least 14% off the cover price. It's quite a bargain! Shipping and handling is just 50¢ per book in the U.S. and 75¢ per book in Canada.* You may cancel at any time, but if you choose to continue, every month we'll send you 6 more books, which you may either purchase at the discount price or return to us and cancel your subscription.

*Terms and prices subject to change without notice. Prices do not include applicable taxes. Sales tax applicable in N.Y. Canadian residents will be charged applicable taxes. Offer not valid in Quebec. All orders subject to credit approval. Books received may not be as shown. Credit or debit balances in a customer's account(s) may be offset by any other outstanding balance owed by or to the customer. Please allow 4 to 6 weeks for delivery. Offer available while quantities last.

◄ If offer card is missing write to: The Reader Service, P.O. Box 1867, Buffalo, NY 14240-1867 or visit www.ReaderService.com ►

## BUSINESS REPLY MAIL
FIRST-CLASS MAIL    PERMIT NO. 717    BUFFALO, NY

POSTAGE WILL BE PAID BY ADDRESSEE

**THE READER SERVICE**

PO BOX 1867

BUFFALO NY 14240-9952

NO POSTAGE
NECESSARY
IF MAILED
IN THE
UNITED STATES

She whimpered...then grabbed one of his hands from the steering wheel, putting it between her legs. His fingers flexed and she gasped, shuddering, her thighs clenching him.

He groaned. "Screw it. I know a place."

He turned off, taking them in an opposite direction, until they reached a secluded part of Golden Gate Park.

"Here?" she squeaked. This was the sort of place where murderers hung out, and thieves. It was stupid, dangerous, undoubtedly...

He got out of the car, surprising her. "I've always wondered about this," he said, pulling her up and out of the car. "I used to work here one summer... I know this place."

She didn't say anything as he led her to a shady grove. He tried the lock. It opened.

"Same combo," he laughed, then tugged her inside.

It was an arboretum of some sort. Fragrant flowers perfumed the air—the slight breeze made the leaves of the tall eucalyptus rustle, and the jasmine flowers bloomed. The sky was clear. There was no one else around.

He pressed her to a tree, removed her top. She felt the smooth bark against her back, then gasped as he undid her bra. "Scott," she said, starting to protest, until he took one breast into his mouth and started to suckle. She arched her back, tilting her pelvis toward him like a flower reaching for the sun.

He tugged her pants and panties down, ruthlessly, leaving her naked. She tugged at his fly, opening it, letting his cock spring free. He dove into a pocket, tearing open the package and hastily slipping the condom on.

Then he plunged inside her, and she let out a loud, "Yesss…"

She hung her legs over his hip bones, urging him deeper, further inside her. The feel of his full cock filling her made her shiver with pure, unadulterated lust. She clawed at his bare shoulders, biting his neck as he gripped her waist, cupped her ass, pulling her tight against his driving thrusts.

The first time she came, she let out a low scream. The second time, she was panting so hard she could barely catch her breath. And when his rocking turned wild, almost chaotic, a third orgasm ripped through her as a complete surprise, a trembling aftershock that turned into a full-blown quake.

He kissed her once, twice, collapsing against her.

"Oh, my God," she said, when she could finally form a coherent sentence. "I think I'm addicted to you."

She hadn't meant to say that out loud. But he let out an uneven laugh.

"I thought you could only be addicted to bad things."

As he slipped out of her, she wondered at his words. He wasn't a bad thing, she thought.

Unless she fell in love with him…and he didn't fall for her. That would be a hell of a lot more than a "bad thing."

# 8

IT WAS AN EARLY MEETING, by Player's Club standards...
midnight on a Sunday. Since Scott had been up until
four the previous night after his Debauchanalia dancing debut, he was starting to feel a tad crispy around
the edges. His work hadn't suffered—yet—but he was
feeling all thirty-four of his years.

Lincoln was talking to those Players that were
paying attention. George and his crew of about seven
were holding up the bar, doing shots and making heck-
ling comments. Lincoln was ignoring them, speaking
with his usual low, casual tone.

"So Tony's doing the marathon," he said, reading
off a list from a black leather portfolio. "He's conned
Victor and Fahey to go with him—twenty-six miles,
that's impressive."

The guys in question grinned, nudging each other.

"Jack, Damon and Bill are BASE jumping in Ari-
zona next week," Lincoln continued. "And Phil's pulling together a group going to Africa. Photo safari.
Anyone wants in, talk to him. Okay, that covers our
latest—"

"We're doing a pub crawl," George yelled, and his cronies chuckled. "Everything over one-twenty proof, and the last guy standing pays the limo driver. Starts Thursday at ten at my house!"

Lincoln took a deep breath, waiting until the laughter died down. "Okay. Let's hear from our latest pledge." He looked pointedly at Scott.

Scott nodded. "I did my second challenge."

That seemed to cut the laughter off at the knees. "What?" George yelped, standing up, his face turning red. "Bullshit. I was at that party. I would've known if you got past a bouncer."

"Oh, really?" Lincoln asked mildly. "Why is that?"

George's face was as red as his hair.

"Was it maybe because you gave Scott's description to the head of security, warning them that he'd try to sneak in?" Lincoln never yelled, never raised his voice a decibel…but the tight smile on his face and the glare in his eyes, were more menacing than all George's bluster. "You forget—I'm friends with most of the bouncers in the city, George. And that was dirty pool."

George gritted his teeth, taking a step toward Lincoln. Lincoln didn't back down an inch.

"I still call bullshit," George said. "Where's his proof?"

For the first time, Scott was glad that Tina had emailed the photos. He showed his phone to George and Lincoln.

"What the hell?" George said. "You were on stage?"

"I said I wanted to crash a party," Scott said. "I did. I got in there. I even performed."

"I'll say," Finn said with a low whistle and a laugh. The others joined in...even a few of George's friends.

George shook his head. "Okay. I guess you pulled it off."

Scott felt his shoulders unknot a little. He didn't know what George's problem with him was, but he was getting sick of being on the defensive around the guy.

"So there's only the running of the bulls left," Lincoln said, and shut his portfolio. "Okay. Next meeting is—"

"Wait a sec," George said, and Scott suppressed a groan. "I've got some new business to discuss."

"Oh?" Lincoln stared at him, one eyebrow kicking up.

"Yeah. Before I left, I sent out an email with a link," George said, and he sounded...well, sneaky. Scott immediately felt wary. "You and I don't see eye to eye, Lincoln, but we both agree that people who put the Club out in the public get kicked out."

Finn nodded. "That's true, Linc."

Lincoln folded his arms. "What's your point, George?"

A few of the guys were checking on smart phones. Faces were grim.

"We were mentioned in a blog," George said, his expression one of smarmy self-righteousness. "One of our guys here. Phil."

Phil, of the aforementioned Africa trip, looked irritated. "I didn't name names."

"You said enough," George shot back. "Anybody with half a brain could tell what you were referring to.

And judging by the number of comments and hits you got, I'd say you were definitely bragging."

"Is this true?" Lincoln asked. He sounded disappointed.

"I... Well, sort of," Phil said, sounding disgruntled. "I was just trying to get more guys on board with the Africa thing. I didn't mean to point fingers at us."

Finn was looking on his phone. He showed the site to Lincoln, who scanned the text quickly.

Then Lincoln sighed. "This is pretty serious, Phil."

"You know the rules," George said, gleeful.

"Fine." Lincoln glanced at the crowd. "All in favor of kicking Phil out, raise your hand."

There was some grumbling, an undercurrent of distress. About half the guys raised their hands.

"It's a tie," Lincoln said. Then he looked at Scott. "You didn't vote."

"He's not a Player!" George protested. "He can't vote!"

"We need a tiebreaker." Lincoln's smile was ghostly. "So...what do you think, Scott?"

Scott swallowed hard. "Maybe... Hell, everybody makes mistakes. I think a second chance isn't a bad thing."

"Spoken like a true *pussy,*" George spat out, and his crew grumbled with him. Phil glared at them, then nodded in gratitude to Scott.

"If that's all..." Lincoln continued, but George interrupted him again.

"As long as I've got the floor, I want to discuss our meeting places," George said, standing up like a politician. "I'd like to suggest a few party places that I think are way cooler than the hole in the walls you've been setting up, Lincoln. And I want to bring strippers back into it. Real strippers. Not burlesque dancers or whatever the hell you call them."

Lincoln grinned. "Majority rules, remember? And you don't have a majority, so maybe you should just sit down."

"Maybe the guys are sick of your little *Dead Poets Society* self-help crap," George growled, getting into Lincoln's face. "Maybe they just want to be studs and have fun for a change, am I right?"

There was a ragged, masculine cheer, mostly from the drunken, rich frat contingent.

"Maybe," George added in a low voice, under the noise of the cheer, "it's time for new management."

"You don't have the brains or the balls to run this thing," Lincoln said dismissively.

"Watch me." George turned around. "Okay, guys, meeting's over. New location'll be announced. Get the hell out!" He was laughing as he and his friends exited.

Lincoln turned to Finn. "He's making his move."

"I didn't think he would," Finn said, sounding irritated...and worried.

"This isn't what I signed on for," Lincoln said.

"Why can't you just kick him out?" asked Scott.

"Wish it were that easy," Lincoln said. "We've all been friends for a long time. Sure, there are some that I like less than others, but when we started, it wasn't like this. Wasn't so polarized." He sighed, rubbing at his temple with one hand. "At least we know it's happening."

"I'd like to do something to help, if I could," Scott offered.

"Make it through the challenges. Help us keep a majority, until we can convince some of the guys he's fooled to come back to reality," Lincoln said. "He just wants a bunch of flunkies to make him look cool. Sometimes he impresses them with stuff, like expensive gifts. Sometimes women."

"He didn't used to be such a dick," Finn said. But even he sounded doubtful.

"Can't you kick him out for the stupid business cards?" Scott asked.

"No proof he's handing them to anybody but pledges," Lincoln said, but rolled his eyes.

Finn exhaled heavily. "George is my cousin. I got him in here. I don't want to kick him out...not unless there's no other choice."

Scott sighed, too. Now, not only was he trying to get into this Club—he was trying to help his new friends, his *cool* friends, who needed him to keep the Club something awesome, and not another drunk, rich party boy's ego trip.

They were *counting* on him.

Scott thought it was worth it...but at this point, he wasn't quite sure. And the "not sure part" was probably what was going to sink him.

SINCE SCOTT WAS WORKING late that Tuesday night, Amanda had decided to have a girl's night in. Between her nascent career as a burlesque dancer, and hanging out with Jackie without divulging either her dancing secret *or* her plot to join The Player's Club, she was almost exhausted. She'd always been a hard worker. Though this whole having-an-outside-life thing was more tiring than she'd expected.

*Of course, it's not the stress of falling for your "fling" adventure guy.*

It wasn't what she was supposed to do. It certainly wasn't what she'd *planned* to do. And even though she knew it was the stupid thing, she wasn't entirely sure it was something she could do anything about. She was falling in love with Scott Ferrell. The man who apparently went to raves and went camping in the Mojave, who went skydiving and God knows what else.

The man who regularly crept onto her fire escape and ravished her. Who'd made love to her in a public place.

The man who was making her no promises.

How in the world was she supposed to keep a man like that interested, much less in love?

*Not thinking about it.* He told her he would be doing a lot of overtime, getting ready for his last big challenge in Spain. She felt a little bereft, she needed to distract herself. She was wearing a baggy T-shirt that had chocolate stains on it, plaid flannel boxer shorts and a pair of superfuzzy socks. She was just going to veg out on the couch: she had a bunch of kettle corn, straight from the farmer's market. She had the makings for killer meatball sandwiches, a messy, delicious, utterly indulgent treat.

There was a *Twilight Zone* marathon on the science fiction channel, completing her version of decadent, introverted, nerdy bliss. She sighed happily, snuggling into her couch.

The familiarly creepy introduction music was just coming on when she heard the knock at her door. Irritated, she got up, looking out her peephole.

It was Scott. He had his jacket slung over his shoulder, a slight growth of beard darkening his jaw. The combination of the suit and the rugged shadow made her mouth water.

"Damn!" Her heart started beating faster. She glanced down at her ratty ensemble. He couldn't see her like this. She didn't even have makeup on.

She quickly darted to her bedroom, tore off the offending articles, and opted to just throw a silk robe on, naked. She ran her fingers through her hair, hoping it wasn't too crazed looking, and wondered how women managed to have that sexy, tousled "bed head" while she just looked as if she'd rubbed her hands on one of those lightning balls.

He knocked again, and she opened the door. "Um, hi," she said, hoping she sounded breathless-sexy, and not just frazzled. "I thought you had to work late tonight."

He grinned, and her heart fluttered. "Bomb threat," he said. "They sent us all home, so I thought I'd stop by." He leaned down, kissing her softly. "I wanted to see you. *Needed* to see you," he whispered against her lips.

She pressed her body against his, sighing into him. How could a woman *not* fall in love with a man who said stuff like that?

He pulled away. "Maybe we should shut the door." He sounded out of breath, too.

Wordlessly, she tugged him inside, shutting the door

and locking it. She was about to kiss him again when he sniffed, and she heard his stomach growl. "What is that? It smells great."

"That? Oh. That's, uh, meatballs. For meatball subs." A completely unromantic meal, she realized. "You're hungry, huh?"

He was staring at her when he answered. "Absolutely," he drawled.

He wasn't looking at the meatballs.

She blushed, and felt her thighs twitch. Then his stomach growled again, and they both chuckled.

"I made plenty," she offered, then frowned. "I've got to warn you—your suit is going to probably take a beating. These aren't the neatest things in the world."

"Some things are worth risking." He winked at her.

She smiled back, heading for the kitchen. Of course he wouldn't care about stuff like that. He had nothing to prove. Besides, he probably ate a lot more neatly than she did. She just didn't pay attention when she ate, it seemed—she always wound up with a spot of coffee on her favorite blouse or wine stains on the sleeve of a sweater.

She made a hefty meatball sub on the homemade French rolls she'd baked that afternoon. A quick pass under the broiler left mozzarella cheese dripping over the meatballs and tomato sauce. She walked out into the living room.

He was on the couch, munching from the large bowl of kettle corn as he watched TV. He'd taken off his shirt. She'd seen his chest plenty of times before, but she always held her breath a little every time she saw it fresh. He looked yummier than all the food in her house. Possibly than all the food in the city—and in San Francisco, that was saying something.

"I love the old episodes of *Twilight Zone*," he said.

She didn't speak. Her mouth was dry.

Then he laughed, a warm, rough sound. "I took off the shirt. Didn't want to get it messed up."

She smiled, putting the tray of food on the coffee table. She was suddenly hungry herself. Ravenous. "You know, those are nice slacks," she said. "Probably dry-clean only."

His answering smile was wicked. "You're right. No sense courting danger."

He stood up, stripping out of his pants, leaving him only in his boxers. She could see his erection tenting the fabric, and she nervously licked her lips.

She sat next to him on the couch, both of them ignoring their sandwiches. He stroked her cheek...then let his fingers trail lower, tugging at the belt of her robe.

"This looks nice, too," he remarked, his eyes gleaming. "You probably don't want to get any tomato sauce on that, either, right?"

She shook her head, unable to speak as he opened the robe, slipping it off her shoulders. He ran his fingertips down her bare shoulder. Her nipples tightened.

"Th-those boxers look nice," she said, not even noticing them. "Maybe we should..."

He stretched out on the couch, and she pulled them off. His cock stood at attention.

She muted the television, and stared at him, her body already beginning to go damp and willing. "Are you starving?" she asked, sending a quick glance over at the sandwiches.

He reached for her. "Only for you."

"Good answer."

She covered him, reveling in the feel of his hot, smooth skin against hers. She kissed him, and he parted her lips, his tongue probing soft and intent as he smoothed his palms up her sides, down her back, cupping her buttocks and molding her more precisely against him. She groaned as she felt the feverish skin of his cock pressed against her stomach, his shaft like a heated bar of iron against the juncture of her legs. She gently gripped his shoulders, pressing her breasts more firmly to his chest as their tongues intertwined. He groaned against her mouth, and she slipped her legs on either side of his hips. The feel of his hardness brushing against her inner thighs made her shudder, her pussy going wet in a rush. She toyed with him, teasing his erection with her entrance, until he growled, his hands jetting to her hips, guiding her directly to the tip of his arousal. She sat up, pushing herself gently over his staff, feeling his cock stretch and fill her as she moaned softly in appreciation. When she was fully impaled on him, she arched her back, enjoying the sensations. When she looked down, he was smiling at her, stroking her, reaching up to cup her breasts, his thumbs circling her erect nipples.

It felt like heaven. She raised her body slowly, then inched lower, setting the tempo, intent on the glide of her flesh over his. His shaft dragged at her clit, and she bit her lip at the delicious sensation. She could feel him brushing against the inside of her pussy, and she gyrated her hips slowly, eager to intensify the secret caress.

It felt like hours, in the best possible way. Her breathing went choppy and ragged as the pleasure seeped into her, drenching every emotion and every physical sensation. He was lifting his hips from the couch to penetrate her more fully, and she was thrusting downward, urging him deeper inside her.

"Baby, please."

He gripped her hips, pulling her tight and flush against his straining hips, and she felt him fill her almost painfully, her clit getting just the pressure it needed. She bucked against him, her speed and rhythm going from slow and graceful to fast and out of control. She ground her hips against his, and he thrust up, pulling her to him, the two of them sweating and straining to reach release.

She felt it first, the climax exploding inside her. She cried out incoherently as her body shuddered, clenching at his cock. He yelled in response, his hips jerking against her, and she collapsed on top of him, their bodies a synchronized mass of shivers and aftershocks. She couldn't hear anything but their rasping breaths, and the thundering beat of her heart, echoed by the thudding pulse of his heart, beating against her ear as she lay pressed against his chest.

After long moments, they got up, straightened out. She quickly got towels, helped them get in some kind of order. Then they sat on the couch, naked and companionable.

The *Twilight Zone* marathon was still running, she realized. It seemed sort of silly.

"This is so awesome," he said, reaching for the sandwich she'd made. "Just what I need. Thanks for feeding me."

She grinned happily as she turned the sound back on. It seemed impossible. This guy was too good to be true.

Of course, maybe she was making it too easy for him. And why should she turn herself inside out, just to please him, right?

He looked at her. "You're hungry, right?"

She stopped, startled. "Well…yeah."

"Then eat," he said, nudging the plate toward her. "And stop thinking. I can practically hear you from over here."

She glared at him, but just for a moment. Then she took a bite of her sandwich. It tasted just as good as she expected it to.

She squealed as a fat blob of sauce hit her thigh. "Crap," she muttered through a mouthful of food, reaching for some napkins.

"No, please. Allow me."

She squealed again when he leaned down, licking the offending spot thoroughly. When he was done, he was grinning at her mischievously.

She swallowed, feeling the sugary heat that he always managed to provoke in her. Maybe he was right. She *was* thinking too much. She should just enjoy it, for what it was, for as long as it lasted. That meant no more trying to impress him. No more trying to be what she thought would keep him in her life and in her bed.

This was probably going to end in disaster. So she would enjoy today while it lasted.

# 9

SCOTT COULDN'T BELIEVE how well his life was going. He was doing stuff with the Players at least once a week—mountain biking one afternoon, kayaking the next, hitting an after-hours party during the workweek. He also had a hot, wonderful woman who blew his mind—both in bed and out of it—on a regular basis. Even his job as a data analyst was going along smoothly, despite all he was juggling. Granted, he was feeling a bit like an impostor, wondering when someone was going to rip off his mask. He wasn't as daring or as suave as he probably should be, given he was pledging The Player's Club. And Amanda seemed to be under the misguided impression that he was some sort of International Man of Mystery, thanks to his late-night shenanigans.

*Oh, yeah. Me and Austin Powers. Yeah, baby.*

Still, while stressful, he had to admit being mistaken for a cool guy, with a cool club and a to-die-for girlfriend, was a nice change.

He was pretty sure his cover had been blown when he hunkered down on her couch, popcorn in hand and watching the *Twilight Zone* marathon with her. The really funny thing was, she thought he was indulging *her*. He probably would have been doing the same thing if he'd been alone that night. The fact that their geek-ness matched was a bit of a charge, too.

"Ferrell. You got those reports?"

Scott looked up. It was Rich, from Sales. Rich schmoozed the clients using the information Scott pulled together, and because of that, and the fat commission checks Rich got and Scott didn't, Rich tended to treat all the data analysts as geeks. Otherwise, Rich was a nice enough guy, he supposed, although Rich had made some inappropriate remarks about Kayla when Scott was dating her. Maybe Scott was a bit prudish, but it wasn't cool to say to a guy how much you'd like to "tap" his girlfriend's ass. Granted, it was the Christmas party, and Rich had been quite plastered. Still, it was the principle of the thing. Consequently, Scott was always a bit leery when Rich came around.

It was also, incidentally, the reason why Scott never got drunk. Alcohol could be worse than truth serum in the wrong hands.

"Guess you've moved on from Kayla, huh?" Rich asked with a note of speculation.

*Why do we keep having Kayla conversations?* Did the guy want to know if the field was clear to ask her out, or something? Ugh. No class. Any of the Players would have known better. Scott shrugged. "I guess," he answered as casually as possible.

"Really went the other direction, huh?"

"What?" Scott finally focused on Rich, who seemed more than curious. "I'm sorry, what'd you say?"

"Not in a bad way," Rich assured him. "I mean,

Kayla's smokin' hot, so you probably wanted a break, someone more in your, you know, league…"

"What the hell are you talking about?" Scott snapped, pushing away from his desk. He moved toward Rich.

Rich obviously sensed the menace in Scott's voice because he held his hands up in the universal calm-down, don't-punch-me gesture. "Whoa! I'm not saying your new girl isn't hot! She's just, you know, more like a schoolteacher than a vixen like Kayla. Still, I'll bet when she lets her hair down…"

Scott barely stopped himself from grabbing the guy by his shirt. Rich seemed to put that together as well, quickly shutting up. "How do you know Amanda?"

Rich swallowed visibly. "She's… Well, ah, she's at reception. In the, er, lobby."

"Amanda's *here?*" Scott blanched. Not that he minded seeing her, even without warning but… "Why didn't Tricia tell me? Call me?"

Rich followed like a puppy when Scott stalked past him, headed for the entrance to the building. "A meeting just got out, and Tricia had to clean up the conference room, so there wasn't anybody at the desk."

"And you just happened to be hanging around," Scott finished.

"Yeah." Rich paused. "And, uh, so were a few of the sales team."

*Great.* Just great. He could just imagine what those jerks were regaling her with. He stopped just short of the lobby when he heard their voices, obviously laughing over the tail end of some story.

"You're saying Scott picked you up at a rave?"

Scott skidded to a halt. "Oof," Rich muttered as he ran into him.

Scott heard Amanda's voice, throaty and low. "Sort of," Amanda demurred.

"Scott. *Our* Scott?" This from John Thompkins, a top selling exec who had no use for the analysts… unless he needed a report done ASAP. His voice dripped with skeptical derision. "I thought Scotty was in bed every night by ten." There was an answering burst of chuckles at that one.

"Who says he isn't?" Amanda responded. The laughter at that one was even louder.

"I meant with like a glass of warm milk," John said. What a dick. He'd make sure Thompkins's next "rush" report got pushed to the bottom of the pile.

"Believe whatever you want," Amanda replied. Her tone screamed her skepticism.

"Well, I used to date him," a feminine voice drawled. "So I ought to know."

Scott winced. That was Kayla. God, could this get any worse?

He stepped forward just as Kayla was saying, "I mean, Scott and I only dated for six months, but I never—"

"Amanda," Scott interrupted, and Kayla at least had the grace to appear embarrassed. "I wasn't expecting you. You weren't waiting long?"

Amanda shook her head, her eyes twinkling merrily. "Don't worry," she said, kissing him softly but thoroughly on the lips. "I was…entertained while I was waiting."

"I'll bet." He glared at the handful of people from

the sales team, including Kayla. The men fled, but Kayla's eyes narrowed with irritation. "Why don't we grab some lunch?" he offered.

"But I'd like to see your office," Amanda protested mildly. "If you don't mind."

"Uh, okay," he said, moving her past a frowning Kayla. "It's not very exciting, though."

"I've never worked in an office," Amanda answered brightly. "So it's always interesting to me to see people who do."

"Never worked in an office? Really?" Kayla pounced. "What *do* you do?"

Amanda returned Kayla's catlike smirk with a wide, genuine smile of her own.

"Lots of different things," she said. "But right now, I'm a stripper."

Every single person within earshot suddenly went silent at Amanda's announcement. Rich, who was lingering nearby, gaped openly.

"My office is this way." Scott quickly hustled Amanda away from the lobby, but not before a bunch of people peeked out of office doors and over cube walls, trying to get a good look at her. He shut his office door behind her, thankful for the first time that his office wasn't the type with windows.

She burst out laughing, quickly covering her mouth to muffle the sounds. When she regained her composure, she grinned at him, slightly sheepish. "Sorry. Maybe I was exaggerating there, but that woman was bugging the hell out of me."

"No problem."

Amanda looked apologetic. "I guess I blew your cover."

"My cover?" Scott said, confused.

"They actually think you're boring." Amanda chuckled.

"Imagine that." Scott cleared his throat.

"They don't know you at all, do they?" She sounded fascinated. "Not about the Club, obviously. But they don't even have any idea what you're really like."

"Amanda, I'm not really all that exciting."

She blinked at him. "Are you serious?"

He shrugged, feeling a little relief as he tugged her to his desk. She leaned on it, and he held her shoulders. "As far as they're concerned, I'm just an analyst, Amanda. I didn't date a whole lot…"

"Yeah, but I saw *who* you dated," she interjected, rolling her eyes.

She had a point there: Kayla was a lot to take in on first meeting. "My life sounds exciting, but it's really no big deal."

She stopped him impatiently. "Okay. Were you or were you not skulking around on my fire escape at three o'clock in the morning when we first officially met?"

"That was different."

"And have you or have you not gone skydiving?"

"Well, yes…"

"Did we practically have sex in a stairwell at a rave?"

He felt heat at the memory. "Definitely. But—"

"Did you get a lap dance on stage at a ten-thousand-dollar-a-ticket party?"

He grinned.

She leaned back against his desk. "Did you break into an arboretum at Golden Gate Park and have sex with me against a tree?"

He straightened a little. "Absolutely," he said, moving a little closer.

"Do any of those things sound boring?"

"No," he remarked, feeling both triumphant and like an idiot. "I mean, when you put it that way."

She smiled, and then her eyes turned mischievous. She hopped up, sitting on his desk. "Does your door have a lock?"

"What?"

"Your office door," she purred, her hands gliding down his shirt and lingering on the button of his fly. "Does it lock?"

He smiled, then took a step away from her, locking his door with a soft click. He stepped back into her embrace, noticing that she'd worn a relatively prim knee-length skirt. He eased the hemline up onto her thighs.

She wasn't wearing underwear. He went fully hard in a rush.

"You're the most exciting woman I've ever met," he said hoarsely as she undid his pants, unzipping the fly and nudging the waistband of his pants and boxers down. His cock sprang from the constraining fabric. She parted her legs wider, and he stepped between them, easing himself into her tight, wet passage. She sighed, long and loud, shivering against him when he buried himself fully.

"You're amazing," he whispered, nipping her jawline

as he eased himself out a little, then pressed forward with a strong, gliding motion.

"Shh," she murmured, her thighs clamping against his hips. "You feel so good…"

They clung to each other, his hips moving in a slow, maddening rhythm against her as his cock slid in and out of her, withdrawing almost fully before delving deep. She gasped every time their bodies connected. He reached between them, stroking her hard, erect clit, and she cried out softly.

"I have to warn you," he murmured against her ear, taking a quick nip on her earlobe. "The walls here are really thin."

"I don't care," she breathed, tilting her head back and arching her hips to take him in even deeper. He clutched her ass, pulling her hard against him as he rocked with more insistent force inside her. She moaned softly, driving him wild. He could feel her squeezing around him, scooting to get closer to him, her legs wrapped around his waist, her hands clutching at his shoulders as she made those soft, incoherent mewling sounds of pleasure.

Soon, he could feel the building pressure of her orgasm as her body clenched around him, her breathing going fast and choppy. He moved quicker, with less finesse and more power. They kissed hard and hot and frenzied, their bodies so close together at times he couldn't tell where he ended and she began, a cliché he'd heard but had never actually experienced until now. He didn't care that they were in his office. They could've been on the fifty yard line of the Super Bowl—he only cared about the amazing, passionate woman who was driving him past the point of reason, burning him alive.

When she came, she let out a moan of pleasure, shuddering against him. Her pussy stroked his fully embedded cock, milking him, clutching around him like a fist, and he came like a shotgun, the pressure and intensity making his mind a complete blank. He trembled against her, his body shivering almost violently. He held her, the two of them kissing, stroking each other, as if they couldn't bear to let go.

Slowly, he came to his senses. He got a good look at her.

"You're all sweaty," he remarked, pushing her now-damp bangs out of her eyes. "But beautiful."

"They're going to know what we did," she murmured, with a rueful but still-mischievous grin. "Do you mind?"

He shrugged. "It's about time they figured out who I really was, I guess."

She kissed him, and he kissed her back, knowing that being with her had a huge amount to do with who he now felt he was.

But what if he didn't make it into the Club? What if he couldn't get her into the Club?

And the thought that kept him up nights—why would she care about him, if she knew what a boring, *normal* guy he was?

THAT EVENING, SCOTT WAS EAGER to get back to Amanda. To his surprise, he got a call first from George. Player's business, he'd said. It surprised him because it was George and George was not exactly interested in business.

The fact they were meeting in a bar, even a classy place like Martuni's, did not surprise him, since George was orchestrating it. When he got there and it was only the two of them, Scott knew he'd been duped.

*What does he want with me?* Scott thought.

"Hey, man. Let me buy you a drink," George said magnanimously from a bar stool, gesturing for Scott to join him. There wasn't a big crowd, and Scott hoped he could get this over with quickly. "What'll you have?"

"Club soda."

"No, really. I'm buying," George pushed, as if somehow Scott couldn't afford something alcoholic. *What an idiot.* "Or maybe you don't know anything about martinis. Tell you what, I'll get you something."

"No, I'm not—"

"Bartender, get this guy a dirty martini, Stoli." His tone was peremptory, and he didn't even look at the man behind the bar. Scott winced as the bartender gave George a second look. Scott hoped his own expression was apologetic enough to forgo anything the guy might do in retaliation—say, put something nasty in his drink.

He sat next to George. "You haven't even pretended to like me," he said, his voice flat. "You've been telling me I won't make the cut, that I'm not fit to be a member. Then you call me up and say you've got something I need to know. What the hell, man?"

George blinked at him. "Couldn't you have at least waited until… Okay, yeah, here's your drink." The now-surly bartender put the drink in front of Scott.

"And hey, I need a refill." George nudged an empty glass away from himself.

Scott rubbed at his temples. The sooner he could get away from this guy, the better.

"Now, what were we talking about?" George's dull eyes sharpened a little, and his expression turned shrewd. "Oh, yeah. Hey, I was just messing with you. It's hazing. It's supposed to be like that, you know?"

"You're supposed to be a dick?"

"Of *course* I am," George said, as if Scott had proven his point. "That's what drives me nuts about Lincoln. He makes it seem like some kind of boring, stupid nineteenth-century men's club. When I joined up, I thought it was going to be a bunch of guys having a good time, you know? Doing crazy stuff, partying. Then Lincoln had to come up with a bunch of rules, and a *philosophy,* and next thing you know, we're turning into a bunch of pussies, I swear."

Scott decided to drink the martini. It burned at his throat, and tasted like ashes—hence the dirty, he surmised. It was probably a good martini if you weren't a dedicated beer drinker. "Again, what did you need to tell me?"

"I need to see where you stand." The bartender put George's new drink in front of him, and he grabbed it blindly, taking a strong swig. "Lincoln's driving the club into the ground, and it seems like every new recruit is just as wimpy as he is."

"I don't think running with the bulls is necessarily wimpy," Scott said mildly, thinking, *Insane, yeah, but not wimpy.*

George rolled his eyes. "Yeah, yeah. Whatever. But

I'm not looking to get killed every year. Especially not with a bunch of *guys,* you know?"

"Lincoln's a friend," Scott said, his voice icy.

George snickered. "Yeah, right." His gray eyes narrowed. "What the hell do you know about him, anyway?"

Scott started to answer, then stopped abruptly.

Actually, he knew next to nothing about Lincoln. Or anybody else on the "crew," for that matter. His brow furrowed.

"Exactly," George said in a low voice. "You don't know these people. They're not really your friends. Lincoln's got a past that nobody knows about. Hell, I used to think he was in some kind of witness protection program. I don't think Lincoln's even his real name."

Scott blinked. "You're crazy."

George shook his head. "Seriously. You try looking into the guy's past, see what *you* come up with."

"Well, I know about Finn's past," Scott said, trying to deflect some of his new concerns. "He's from a famous family, and…"

George's guffaw cut him off. "Yeah. He's from *my* family," he said, and the bitterness in his voice was palpable. "You wouldn't even recognize him. That's why I thought we were on to something good. But Lincoln turned the thing into some kind of…self-help group. And Finn buys every damned word the bastard says."

Scott shifted uncomfortably on the bar stool. He didn't believe George—the guy was far too shady to be taken at face value. But the points he was bringing up did make him question, a little, what he was getting into.

"They could kick you out, you know. For breaking any one of their precious 'rules.' Talk shit about another member? They can say you're holding a grudge, and boot you out. Don't attend enough of their 'adventure' exercises? You're not playing the game in the field, or the park, or whatever stupid-ass metaphor Lincoln's come up with. And bam, they boot you out."

"I don't think it's that easy," Scott demurred.

"Oh, really?" George's look was pure derision.

"No," Scott continued, "or else they'd have gotten rid of you."

"They can't get rid of me," George said scornfully, drinking the rest of his martini and gesturing to the bartender again. "I was there when there was only like five members, and I'm Finn's cousin. They wouldn't dare."

"So, is this all the information you wanted to give me?" Scott said. "That Lincoln's a wussy leader with a changed name and no past?"

"Doesn't it bother you?"

Scott frowned. "I don't see how it applies at all. This is just a club, for God's sake. A *hobby*. It's not that big a deal."

George's eyes glinted. "So you don't care if you get kicked out or not? The Club means nothing to you?"

Scott tried to say yes, but found that he couldn't.

"Jeez, you're as pathetic as all the rest of them." George sneered. "You think that this stupid club is going to make you a better man, some kind of frickin' hero or something. Just by camping and hiking and jumping out of planes."

"You're right," Scott said, his temper flaring. "It's

much better to nail a bunch of disposable broads and get hammered every night. Now *that* proves something."

George's face turned red, and a small vein throbbed in his temple. He didn't know how old George was, but anger seemed to add about five years at least.

"Goddamned goody-goody. You, and the rest of them." George threw his credit card down on the bar, and the bartender grabbed it quickly. "I should've known, but no, I thought I'd give you one last chance."

"What difference does it make? Why do you think I'm such a threat?" Scott finally said. "You've gone out of your way to stop me from joining the Club. If I join, so what? Who really…"

Then, suddenly, a bunch of conversations clicked into place.

*We haven't had a new member in a while…*

*If he broke a rule, we'd be able to kick him out…*

"You've been the one preventing new members from joining," Scott said, snapping his fingers. "You think they've finally found a way to prove you're breaking a rule and kicking you out. You're afraid of being replaced as one of the big men on campus. And it's eating you up. Isn't it?"

"You don't know anything," George snarled. "They don't have the balls to kick me out. And if they did, they'd be sorry."

"I'll just bet." Scott stood up. "Thanks for the drink and for the utter waste of time. When I do become a Player, I can almost guarantee that I *will* look for a way to kick you out."

George was too speechless to reply.

"Exactly," Scott said. "Have a nice night."

AMANDA WAS SITTING in her living room with her oldest friend, Jackie, and her newest, Tina. The two women got along better than she'd hoped: Jackie was more oriented toward mosh-pit violence than dancing, and Tina sounded as though she'd had enough dating advice to last her a lifetime, but the two found a common ground.

Namely, the fact that it was time for Amanda to move on from her booty call with Scott.

"It's exciting, and all that, but now it's starting to look a little...well, pathetic," Jackie said, with her usual no-punches-pulled grace.

Tina shrugged. "He was no dancer. You got him into that party because he wanted to get in," Tina said, sounding irritated—not at Amanda, but at Scott. "He's got all the advantages, and you're the one who jumps when he whistles."

"Good grief." Amanda rubbed her eyes. Flings were supposed to be fun, right? When did they institute a rule book? "We have sex. Great sex."

"You," Jackie said, pointing a finger at her, *"have cooked him dinner."*

Tina gasped, shooting Amanda a shocked, accusatory look.

Amanda let out a huff of indignation. "I just cooked *you* dinner, you twerps."

Jackie ignored that point. Tina grinned sheepishly, taking another bite from her brie-and-caramelized-onion on homemade sourdough bread. "You *are* a great cook," she said, smiling happily.

"You cook for a man, you might as well wear a T-shirt that says 'Hi, I'm Interviewing for the Position of Wife.' Honestly," Jackie scoffed, "I ought to write a book."

"You should," Amanda said eagerly, hoping to change the subject.

"She's right, though, hon," Tina said, wiping her hands daintily on her napkin. "Cooking for a man is a husband-trapping exercise. We know it, and they know it. Granted, your cooking could probably land somebody, but it's probably going to just make him take advantage of you."

"Why marry the girl when you can get the grilled cheese for free?" Jackie muttered darkly, before finishing her own sandwich.

"At least I haven't done his laundry," Amanda piped up. "You guys act like I'm invertebrate, I swear to God. I'm not angling to be his wife."

"You want to be his girlfriend, though." Tina got up, clearing away the dishes. Jackie nodded in agreement.

"Okay." She wasn't going to get that one past these two anyway. "Yeah, maybe. It'd be nice. But I've been married, and I don't need to repeat that right away."

"I don't have any problem with you marrying," Jackie amended, her voice growing much more gentle. "Just trying to marry the wrong guy, that's all. If he doesn't want to admit you're his girlfriend, then he's wasting your time."

"Unless I'm *just trying to have some sex*," Amanda said, then threw her hands in the air. "Why do I keep having this conversation? I love you, Jacks, but you really need to save some of it for your advice columns, you know?"

She got up, disgusted with the whole topic, and headed for her kitchen. She'd splurged and made chocolate petits fours, glazed with ganache and filled with raspberry jam and fresh whipped cream. "Have some dessert."

Tina considered her waistline, but indulged in one anyway, making very pleased yummy noises. Jackie considered her tiny, artistic cake carefully. Then she tilted her head. Amanda braced herself for the assault.

"You miss the shop, don't you?"

Amanda blinked. She hadn't thought about the shop in—well, a long time. "Sometimes."

"Not just the shop. Being around food. Being in business."

Amanda shrugged. "Sometimes," she repeated. Now that it had been brought to her attention, she realized that what used to be stress had been replaced with a numb sort of ache. She wasn't sure if that was better.

Jackie turned to Tina. "Maybe it's not the guy, after all," she mused, as if Amanda weren't even there. "Maybe it's the job."

"Oh?" Tina said, pouring a cup of coffee for all of them.

"She's never *not* owned a business. She's always run the show," Jackie said slowly, frowning with thought. "Now she's trying to get a handle on this Scott thing, but I think it's more distraction."

"Feel free to open a forum on my life," Amanda said caustically, unable to even enjoy her dessert. She grabbed a mug of coffee, its warm richness soothing.

"You're the one that told me not to open a business, re-member?"

"You are all or nothing. I should've seen it," Jackie said ruefully. "You're not the type to get a hobby. I guess it was silly to even suggest it."

"All right, that's enough!" Amanda barked, slam-ming her mug down. Tina stared at her, wide-eyed, and Jackie finally gave Amanda her full attention. "Maybe I'm getting too involved with Scott. But that's my prob-lem, my business, and as much as I love you, I'm get-ting tired of being treated like your letter of the week at the advice column."

Jackie looked genuinely wounded. "I was just…"

"Trying to help. I know." Amanda forced her voice to lower. "I know I'm still not happy. And that scares me. But trust me, I'm doing the best I can. Maybe I'll do something food related again, I don't know. I know I need to do something. Something besides having wild monkey sex with Scott," she said, causing Tina to grin. "But I don't know what. And until then…"

Tina stood next to her, nudging her with her hip. "Until then—monkey away, crazy girl. Sorry, I shouldn't have come on so strong. It's just, I've been where you are. Nobody wants to see a friend being used."

*Used.* Was that what Scott was doing?

Or, really, was that what *she* was doing?

Jackie nodded. "I'm glad you pushed back on me. I know I come on too hard. But you need to draw bound-aries with him, too. Otherwise… Well, I'll be here to pick up the pieces when he lets you down, but I swear

I'm going to slash his tires and God help him if I run into him in a dark alley."

Amanda smiled. "Point taken. If it comes to it, I imagine a very violent 'I told you so' in my future."

There was a knock on the door. "Speak of the devil," Jackie muttered darkly.

"I need to get going, anyway," Tina said, giving her a warm hug. "Up for a little club work? Less rowdy this time, I promise. With the whole troupe."

"I'm there," Amanda said, and then she gave a hug to Jackie. "Thanks, guys."

She opened the door. Scott was there, looking harried and tired, and happy to see her. Then he saw her friends and backed up a step, his smile a little hesitant. Tina smiled back. Jackie sent him a third-degree glare and walked past him, saying goodbye to Amanda only. When they'd left, he walked in, wiping his forehead with the back of his hand.

"So your friends hate me, huh?"

"At least you've seen my friends," Amanda said, then bit her lip. "I'm sorry. That was completely uncalled for."

He blinked at her.

"They— My friends don't necessarily think our fling is the healthiest thing for me," she said, washing the dishes quickly.

He leaned against a counter, drying each dish and putting it away without error. He *had* been over for dinner a lot, she admitted. "What do you think? Is this... Are we unhealthy?"

She gripped the edge of the counter by the sink for a minute, closing her eyes. She was tired. The malaise, her general boredom and unhappiness with her new life of leisure had been creeping up on her. She hadn't really brought it into focus until Jackie had commented on it tonight. She didn't want to break up with Scott, although she might have to, sometime.

*But please, not tonight.*

"Maybe," she answered honestly. "But, hey, we've got great sex."

He wrapped his arms around her, kissing her neck. "That we do."

"And not much else."

He froze against her for a second, then continued kissing her shoulder. "I didn't know you wanted something else."

"I didn't say I did," she said, and recognized the petulant sound of her own voice. She sighed. "Do you?"

"I don't know," he said, and his honesty stung. "I do know that we like a lot of the same movies, the same books. We've got similar senses of humor." He turned her to face him. "That's more than sex."

She leaned her forehead against his chest as reality struck her.

*Damn it,* that *was why I wanted to be your girl-friend.*

Because he'd be perfect for her. Her ex-husband had made sense to her on paper, but there had been no passion. Now, she had passion—and insanity.

What she really needed was some kind of happy medium, not a fling with a daredevil who didn't want to commit, just to get into a club that she knew almost nothing about except rumors and what little she learned from Scott.

"Well, before we got all grim," Scott said, stroking her cheek, "I did have a question to ask you."

*Not the question I want you to ask,* she thought, depressingly. "Yes?"

He seemed nervous all of a sudden, and rubbed the back of his neck. She found herself unwillingly curious. "Well, I know I probably should have asked you earlier, but I was wondering…"

"Yes?" she repeated, without enthusiasm.

"Would you like to go to Spain with me?"

She blinked. "Spain?"

"You said you'd help me with my challenges," he quipped, and his broken smile melted her, like it always did. "I've got this bull run to tackle."

"I've always wanted to go to Europe," she murmured. "I'll admit, I hadn't planned on jogging with two-ton bovines to do it, though."

"A wild woman like you can handle it, no sweat," he said with no tone of sarcasm. He grinned at her. Then he kissed her again, deeper, harder. "Come with me," he whispered against her skin.

She thought about it. She had that little plane phobia thing. And the thought of running with the bulls terrified her. And she was falling in love with him—and this was only going to be more torturous when he became a Player, and all she had of him was casual sex and these senseless "adventures."

He nudged her chin until her eyes met his. "Please." There was genuine longing in his gaze—a real plea.

She swallowed. "Yeah. I'll go."

# _10_

SCOTT WAS IRRITATED. It figured that the company would
have a party when he was just finishing all his backlog.
He'd just wrapped up the last report before his vacation, and he still needed to pack.

He glanced at his watch. At least the usual office
parties had been scaled back from lavish sit-down din-
ners with rubbery chicken to uncomfortable cocktail
parties with better hors d'oeuvres and a cash bar. The
company had barely made quota, anyway—not exactly
a huge reason to celebrate. Still, it was a nice restaurant, and there was a lot of mingling. You could see
who was here to "work the room," angling for a better
job in the next reorganization, who was trying to so-
lidify their position, and who was simply putting in an
appearance out of bare courtesy.

Scott fell into the latter camp, big-time.

He glanced at his watch again. The minute hand
still hadn't moved. He could be with Amanda, eating
her fantastic oven-fried chicken with mashed potatoes,
looking at pictures of Spain and discussing what they'd
see. And, of course, making love to her until he was

practically blind and paralyzed from the sheer force of it.

So far, they'd had sex in every room of her apartment—and on almost every surface. The only place they hadn't was the fire escape, frankly because he wasn't quite that adventurous.

Not yet, anyway. Something about that woman seemed to bring out the worst in him...or the best, depending on how you looked at it.

"Scott," his boss, Jake, said. "Glad to see you here."

Scott smiled, shaking his hand. Finally. Now, he could make polite remarks and get the hell out of here.

"Saw you'd put in for vacation. Good to see you're finally taking a break, but I don't know if I can let you go that week. I expect we'll be getting slammed with a lot of reports. The reorganization will probably have happened, and you know how crazy that makes everyone. So how about you shift that, say, to the following week?"

Scott shrugged. "Actually, I have to leave that week. I've already bought plane tickets."

Jake blinked at him, smiling a little...until he realized Scott was serious. "Plane, huh? Where you going?"

"Spain." He left it at that.

"Huh. Europe. Some kind of tour?"

"Something like that." *Actually, I'm going to be chased by a couple of huge herbivores down some cobblestone streets.* Better to keep that little fact to himself. It might sound cool, but it was also sort of stupid out of context.

Okay. Possibly a bit stupid *in* context.

"All right, fine, take the time off," Jake said grudgingly.

"Spain? Did I hear that right?"

Jake turned to see Kayla and some strange guy next to her—probably Kayla's new boyfriend, Scott thought. Funny, that didn't really sting anymore. Kayla's perfectly tweezed eyebrow went up in an aristocratic arch.

"Yup. Our boy's going to Spain on a tour or something," Jake replied.

Put that way, it sounded lame. Scott quickly tried to amend his boss's statement. "I didn't actually say…"

"I love Spain," Kayla's new guy said easily, as if he went there every weekend. He was tall and broad, built like a linebacker, but there was something shrewd about his face that suggested more than "dumb jock." He studied Scott intently. "Where in Spain are you going? Madrid? Lots of good clubs there."

"Like Scott goes clubbing," Kayla said with a wry grin. "Come on, Matt. Let's get going."

"Um, not Madrid," Scott said. "Pamplona."

"Pamplona, huh? In July?" The guy laughed. "You'll probably be able to see those nutcases run with the bulls. That's about the right time."

"You don't say?" Scott suppressed the urge to punch the guy. With everything he'd been through in the club, he felt comfortable with the notion of mixing it up.

"Hey, if you run with the bulls, I want one of those red neckerchief things," Jake joked, nudging Scott on the shoulder.

"I've got to run," Scott said quickly. "I promised a friend I'd—"

"No, don't rush off," Kayla's boyfriend—Matt?—

said, as Jake excused himself and moved to the next knot of people. Kayla looked a bit surprised, as well. Why was her burly boyfriend sticking to him like lint? "Kayla's mentioned you."

"Well, we did used to date," Scott said, to Kayla's obvious discomfort. What, was the guy looking for a user rating or something? *I'd give Kayla three stars as a girlfriend?*

"She mentioned that you've been going through some changes lately," Matt said. "Said you used to be really, you know, quiet and sort of shy, and now you seem to be keeping secrets, acting differently."

"What is this? An intervention?" Scott asked, baffled. "Listen, I don't even know who you are. You don't work with us, do you?"

"I'm sorry. My name's Matt. Matt Richardson." He had a friendly smile, broad and harmless, the human equivalent of a puppy. "Nice to meet you. No, I don't work with you, but I am interested in people. Anyway, she mentioned that you seemed like you were into something. She sounded concerned. I just wanted to find out what was going on."

Kayla? Concerned about *him?* "Well, thanks, but I'm fine."

Matt leaned closer, almost conspiratorial. "Kayla said your girlfriend came to the office, caused kind of a stir. And there's been rumors about you being tired coming in—like you've been having some really late nights." He paused a beat, his tone suggestive, coaxing. "Bunch of new friends, maybe."

"I also told you I couldn't believe it," Kayla said

sourly. "Honestly, Matt, this isn't a story. Why are you being so pushy about this?"

Matt's eyes glittered. "Mr. Ferrell—Scott—have you ever heard about The Player's Club?"

Scott froze, then cleared his throat. "The what?"

"The Player's Club," Matt said, and his voice held a tinge of pure avarice. "It's a group of guys in the city, very hush-hush. Rich, influential guys. They throw parties, but they also do crazy stuff. Skydiving, BASE jumping, white-water rafting." He waited a beat. "Running with the bulls."

"God, you'd have to be living under a rock not to know about those guys," Kayla scoffed. "But…you don't honestly think that Scott's with those people, do you?"

Damn. Was this guy trying to join, or something? Or maybe he had been a member, and this was some sort of confidentiality test?

"I think that maybe he is with those guys," Matt said, his eyes never leaving Scott's face. "Well, Scott?"

Suddenly, something that Kayla said registered in Scott's head.

*Matt, this isn't a story.*

"You're a reporter," Scott said slowly.

Matt grinned. "Guilty as charged."

"And you're looking to write about these guys."

Matt nodded.

"I'm telling you, there's no way Scott's…"

"Kayla's right," Scott said brusquely. "Even if there was a club like this—and I always thought they were some kind of urban legend, like the sewer alligator—I seriously doubt that they'd take someone like me. I'm pretty damned boring. Ask her." He nodded at Kayla, who at least had the grace to look embarrassed.

"You're lower profile—that's what they like," Matt protested. Now that he'd dropped the laid-back pretense, he was clearly hungry, like a shark scenting blood in the water. "At least, that's what I hear they like. But they've been getting a little crazier. Rumor has it they were involved in trashing a nightclub and harassing a bunch of strippers."

Scott frowned. That didn't sound like Lincoln. *George,* he thought, annoyed. If George kept it up, they sure as hell wouldn't be a "secret" society for long.

"They're on the radar, and people love to read about them. If I could get a story, it'd be huge."

"I can't help you."

"If you know anything, I'd make sure you stayed completely anonymous," Matt said, his tone persuasive and as gentle as a wrecking ball. "You wouldn't get in trouble."

"I told you, I'm not a part of this club," Scott said. "And I've got to go. My girlfriend's expecting me."

He started to turn and walk away. Matt took his arm, putting a business card in his hand. "If you change your mind, call me."

Scott shrugged off the guy's hand. A reporter. Jeez. Of all the stupid bad luck.

He headed for the door. There was a time when he'd feel thrilled that a reporter actually thought something in his life was interesting enough to write about. Man, he'd been pathetic. Now the last thing he needed was publicity. He wanted to make it into this club.

Of course, there was a chance that Amanda was only

into him to get into the Club, as well. And because she thought he was one of these daredevil badasses.

*Don't they know who you really are?*

He sighed. He was starting to wonder.

## Why did I agree to this?

It had to be two o'clock in the morning—at least, it was somewhere—though Amanda had no idea exactly where they were. It was dark outside the windows, as far as she could see. She sat in the middle seat, coach class, on a plane headed toward Madrid. She forced herself not to grip the armrests, instead trying to read the paperback romance she'd picked up at the airport. She'd read the same page, over and over, while almost everyone else was snoozing away, seats reclined as much as possible, with those little neck pillows and blankets. They looked blissfully oblivious to the fact that they were, what, forty thousand feet from the ground with nothing but air holding them up.

She forced herself to take a couple of deep breaths. This was bad. This was very, very bad.

Scott touched her arm, and she jumped. "What? What?"

He hushed her, smiling a warm, crooked smile that had her easing her choke hold on the poor, defenseless book. He took it out of her hands. "You could've told me you hated flying."

"I was rather hoping I'd be drunk enough that it wouldn't make a difference."

"How's that working for you?"

She tried for a smile, but got the feeling it just came out looking sickly. "Two tiny bottles of vodka, and the stewardess hasn't been back since. Apparently it's not quite doing the trick."

Scott smiled sympathetically. "I used to hate flying, too."

"Really?" She latched on to any sympathy she could get. "What did you do to cure yourself?"

"I tried going to classes," he admitted in a low whisper, and she could have kissed him. Even if he were lying, which she guessed he was. "Meditation, guided visualization, you name it."

"Then what?"

"Well, I guess I just figured that it wasn't much worse than getting in a bus." He shrugged. "I just sort of got over it."

She sent him a wilting look. "That's not really helping me, Scott."

He smiled, then glanced around. "Looks like everybody's asleep."

"But us," she grumbled.

He leaned close, his lips brushing against her earlobe, his breath tickling her ear. "You know, the key is distraction," he murmured, scarcely audible. "You wouldn't be afraid if you focused on something else."

"You got any suggestions?" she shot back, with a touch of acidity.

He pressed a hot kiss against her neck, and she felt a thrill flutter in her stomach. "I've got a few ideas."

"Hmm." She turned and shivered as he nibbled her neck. "You know, you may be on to something."

He returned to her ear. "Why don't we try the restroom?"

"I'm fine," she demurred, turning back to him. "Why don't we just…"

Then she froze. Her eyes widened. He chuckled wickedly.

"Trust me," he breathed, "in a few minutes, you won't even know where you are."

Good God. Couldn't they get arrested? Or…deported, or something? And those restrooms were *tiny*. She couldn't even imagine…

He reached under her blanket, his hand stroking between her thighs. She went damp.

"Okay," she rasped. "I'll, er, go first."

She headed for the restroom. The flight attendants seemed congregated in the back of the plane, drinking coffee, talking in animated whispers. The first-class section was completely curtained off. Except for a random few people, everyone was asleep.

She crept into the restroom, closing the door behind her. Her heart was pounding in her chest when she heard his soft knock. She opened it, stifling a giggle as he crammed into the compartment with her and locked the door behind him.

His eyes were alight as he reached for her. She kissed him, hard and quick, still giggling softly, breathlessly. "I can't believe we're doing this," she mouthed.

"Better hurry," he whispered back, nipping at her throat. "God, I want you."

She felt adrenaline and lust drenching her body, and she quickly undid her jeans, shimmying them down her legs and off her feet. He undid his pants, and she shoved them down his thighs, bumping against a wall as she did so, which set off a fresh set of strangled chuckles. "Shh!" she breathed, her face splitting with a smile.

Then he reached for her, and all she felt was urgency, need. His cock was already completely erect, pointing at her like a missile, and he pressed her against the wall. She almost fell onto the toilet seat, and she laughed out loud.

He covered her mouth with his, smothering her humorous sounds as he moved between her legs. She wrapped her legs around his waist, feeling either side of the room against the outside of her thighs. She was pretty sure her knee was hitting the counter.

He had rolled on the condom, and now he pressed inside her in a rush, and she was more than ready for him. He groaned softly, so quietly, as he buried himself fully in her, and she tightened her thighs around his waist. He withdrew, then pressed forward, slowly, deliberately.

She rested her chin on his shoulder, and saw her face in the mirror. She almost didn't recognize herself. Her hair, tousled and sexy, just like a model's. Her pale skin flushed. Her eyes were bright as diamonds, and her lips were rosy and swollen from kisses. Scott looked like a mystery man; his face was hidden, his clothes still on, his broad shoulders covering her. He still had a great ass, and watching it clench as he thrust inside her made her wet and shivery and aching with need. He increased his pressure and his speed, and she clutched at him, with her arms and her legs, urging him harder, faster, *now.*

"Scott," she said, her voice barely audible, just a slight brush of air against his neck as she matched his every thrust, shimmying against him, feeling his cock glide against her clit as he moved, stroking the inside of her pussy with his full hardness. She gasped, sounding choppy and urgent. Her hips bucked against his as he continued his sensual onslaught.

"Hurry," she whispered. She could feel the beginnings of orgasm curling around her consciousness, and her pussy started to contract...

Suddenly, there was a knock at the door, and they froze. "Everything all right in there?" a brisk masculine voice asked with concern.

She looked at Scott, terrified even as her orgasm screamed to be released. "Out in just a minute," Scott said, his voice hoarse. Then he pressed his mouth to hers as he slammed into her, a high, perfectly aimed thrust that hit her G-spot and shattered her control.

The taboo, getting caught, everything flooded over her, and her orgasm splintered her into pieces. She screamed soundlessly against his mouth as her pussy rippled around him, her thighs clamping onto him like a vise. She threw her head back, gasping. She hit her head against the wall, and didn't care. He shuddered against her, his body jerking, the two of them gasping and straining with the aftershocks.

Long minutes afterward, sweaty and shaking, he finally set her down. Her legs were too shaky to support her, and she sank down onto the toilet. "Oh, wow," she murmured. "I can't believe we just did that."

Scott's eyes were gleaming mischievously. "Come on. Guy's waiting," he mouthed.

She blushed, quickly trying to tug her pants back on—not an easy feat, considering the crammed quarters. She kicked Scott twice before she finally managed to get clothed again. "What is he going to think?" she asked.

"He's going to wish he was me," Scott answered with a wink. "Don't worry. Just head for the seat. I'm sure this happens all the time."

Scott opened the door, and for a second, he stopped—causing Amanda to bump into his back. "You prick," Scott said, in a low hiss.

She heard masculine laughter, and abruptly wondered what was going on.

"I thought you were sick or something," a man's voice said disingenuously. "You know. Puking."

Scott turned back to her. "Amanda, go on ahead to the seat." He was staring at a man, their age, with carroty-red hair and a smarmy expression. The red-haired man winked at her. She returned to her seat, but the plane was quiet enough that she could catch snippets of their conversation.

"Who was *that?*"

"Not your business, that's who," Scott said sourly.

"Girlfriend?" The man's tone was sarcastic. "Do Lincoln and Finn know about this? And what does *she* know?"

She didn't catch Scott's answer, although she found herself desperately wanting to. Finally, she closed her eyes, waiting for him to return.

He had to be a Player. She wondered how they were going to get around the stricture of him not telling anyone…especially when it came time for her to join.

Her mind was awhirl. Eager, impatiently, she suddenly realized that she was in an airplane, and she couldn't care less.

*Sonofabitch,* she thought. *He really did cure my fear of flying.*

But she wasn't sure if lust or falling desperately, stupidly in love was what did the trick.

# 11

THE FLIGHT WAS OVER, Amanda was grateful, ecstatic to be on the ground and alive…and only a little jet-lagged. They'd been here a day, wandering around, fighting off napping. Now, at night, at a restaurant and dance club, Amanda was seeing a whole new side to Scott. She thought he might rush off, that he might have Player's Club business to attend to. Instead, he told her that they were off doing something, but he'd wanted to spend the time with her.

She wasn't sure if that was romantic, or shady—if he wanted to focus on her or hide her.

"Whoo! Another shot!" he crowed, accepting a shot of the clear liquor they were drinking… Vodka? Grappa? What the heck *was* he drinking?

He sat down next to her with a goofy, endearing smile. "I'm getting plastered, aren't I?"

She nodded. "Is this a regular thing?" Might as well know now.

He shook his head, a little too vigorously, and then he needed to hold the table for balance to get his bearings. He said, slowly and with careful enunciation, "I don't get drunk. It makes you lose too much control."

"Obviously," she said, sipping the same glass of red wine she'd started the night with. "You want any more tapas?" She nudged the plate toward him.

He opened his arms voluminously, almost hitting the people who were sharing their table with them, family style. Considering they were also a bit inebriated, they forgave him easily. "I've had the best food, the best drink and I've got the best girl in Spain," he said, kissing her noisily. "And I'm *running with the bulls tomorrow!*"

Another rowdy cheer at this one. He kissed her more intently. She found it sweet, if disconcerting.

"You've got a big day tomorrow," she said. "Why don't I pour you into bed?"

"I can think of better things we can do there," he said with what he probably thought was a suave bit of eyebrow wiggling.

"Let's just get there first," she said, grinning. "Then we'll see what happens next."

He let her help him out of the restaurant, high-fiving various other tourists and run aficionados on the way out. "I'm so glad you're here," he said, leaning on her heavily.

"I'll bet," she said with a loud *oof.* "You probably couldn't find your way back to the hotel in this state, pal."

He let out a bark of laughter, then shook his head. "No. I mean, I'm so glad you're here with me in Spain."

She felt a burst of warmth in her chest. "I'm glad, too."

"I can't believe I'm here."

"Me neither," she echoed with feeling.

"No, I can believe you're here," he said, scoffing at her remark. "You're an adventurer."

"I am?" She blinked. She'd been called many things, but adventurer was rarely one of them. "Then...what does that make you?"

"Incredibly lucky." She wasn't sure if he was deliberately misinterpreting her remarks or what, but he stood then and cupped her face. "If it hadn't been for you and the Players, I would still be stuck in the same windowless office, watching TV way too late, playing video games and not getting any sleep in my lonely, empty bed."

Now her mouth fell open. "You weren't like that," she protested.

He shook his head. "You don't even really know me. How crazy is that? You think I'm this larger-than-life guy."

"You *are* larger-than-life," she said. "You just aren't giving yourself a chance."

He shook his head, then started heading down the street, until she tugged his arm.

"Wrong way," she corrected gently, guiding him toward their hotel. They trudged in silence for a minute, the mood going from ebullient to deflated in less than sixty seconds. She ushered him up to the room. "So... what did you want to do in bed?"

He collapsed face-first into the pillow. "Try to get the room to stop spinning," she heard his muffled voice say.

She sighed, shaking her head. He obviously didn't drink all that often. It was surprising…and sort of cool.

"How did you get involved with The Player's Club, anyway?"

He rolled over, keeping his eyes closed. "Remember those guys? That night, in the alley?"

"The night I found you on my fire escape?" she asked, feeling fond of the memory.

"The very same. Well, I followed them one night."

She gasped, sitting next to him on the bed. "By yourself? Are you crazy? They could have been… You could have been…"

"Did you ever feel like you were… I don't know. Trapped in your life?" His voice sounded as if he was pleading for her understanding.

She paused, surprised by the turn of conversation. Then she started slowly stroking his hair across his forehead. She thought of her marriage, the chocolate shop. How she'd exchanged *busy* for *happy*.

"Yeah," she said. "I think I know how that feels."

"I was trapped in my life," he said, rolling to his side to stare at her more intently. "I hated just playing it safe. I was so stuck in my life I didn't even know how unhappy I was."

"I'm sorry." The words didn't express enough. She cuddled next to him, and he kissed her temple.

"These guys showed me that. They woke me up to the fact that I was just going through the motions, that I wasn't living my life, I was serving it like a jail sentence. All the crazy stuff—the bull run, the skydiving, all of it—isn't necessarily the stuff that makes me happy. But it was like dynamite. Suddenly, I'm not stuck anywhere. Anything is possible."

She wanted to weep for him. He sounded so broken, and then so hopeful.

"I feel alive now," he said, stroking her face.

She kissed him softly on the lips. "I'm glad."

"How about you?" he asked. "What makes you feel alive?"

"I don't know," she said. "I thought I used to, but...I don't know. I just know that I envy you. I want to live my life deliberately, like you are. That's why I pushed so hard to get you to help me join the Club."

He nodded.

"But I know I feel alive when I'm with you," she added ruefully. "Maybe some of your Player's philosophy is wearing off on me."

He laughed. Then he leaned in, kissing her more intently. His hand stroked up her stomach, cupping her breast. He rolled her onto her back, then kissed her more intently.

"I think I remember what I wanted to do to you," he whispered roughly against her ear.

She could feel his erection pressed like a rod of iron against her thigh. "I think you're up for it," she agreed, surprised.

"Is this blouse a favorite of yours?"

She frowned. "Not particularly. Why?"

He smiled, and his expression was devilish—pure sex, laced with a dark mischief she'd never seen before. She shivered, surprised at how turned on he'd managed to make her in such a short period of time. "Scott..."

He reached down, grabbing her blouse and yanking

it, hard. Buttons went flying as they were torn off the hem. Before she could yelp in protest, he was kissing her chest, suckling her through the lace of her black bra. She gasped, then moaned as her back arched.

He'd always been a thoughtful lover. Considerate. Definitely inventive, and above all adventurous—she'd certainly never had sex in public before he came along. But tonight, he was unleashed. She wasn't a participant so much as she was simply *experiencing* him, like standing in a summer thunderstorm.

He stripped out of his own clothes with surprising grace, then yanked off her skirt. She was wearing a black thong to match the bra—she'd invested in a lot more lingerie since she started seeing Scott—and he didn't take it off. He merely pushed it to one side, pressing inside her with a swift, sure stroke. She moaned, her head moving from side to side as he rode her, lifting her hips to meet him, angling her so her leg rested against his chest, her heel resting on his shoulder. He rippled against her like lapping ocean waves.

The first orgasm was like a lightning strike: brilliant, dazzling, unexpected. She cried out, her hands fisting in the sheets.

He turned her over, unclasping her bra and flicking it off her shoulders. Then he leaned against her, his chest to her back. He cupped her breasts as he entered her from behind. He pistoned against her hips, his cock thick, relentlessly pleasuring her. He moaned as he rode her, and she moaned in response, arching, bucking her hips back to meet his. He spread her legs a little, wriggling somehow, until she felt as if she was on fire with need. Her last coherent thought was, *Did he take a class since the last time we...?*

He hit her G-spot with the tip of his cock, and she cried out, her body clenching against him. She was mewling, all but screaming with the reverberations.

"Still not done with you yet," he growled. He spun her again, lifting her against him, pressing her against the headboard, wrapping her legs around him. It was just like the club, just like the park, one of her favorite positions. His shaft rubbed against her clit in just the right way as he plunged in and withdrew. She took in a quavering, hiccupping breath. "Oh, Scott..." She clawed at his shoulders, mindless with how he was making her feel.

His tempo sped up, going from measured and masterful to animalistically wild. He was almost shouting with it, the bed squeaking in protest at the power of his thrusts. She clung to him. When she came, she screamed. He echoed it, shuddering against her, his hips jerking like a shot cannon. They sank to the bed, still joined.

"Wow," she murmured, when she could finally speak.

His eyes were closed—he had to be already asleep. She kissed him again, holding him for a moment.

"I love you," she whispered.

She didn't think he heard her, but his hold on her tightened.

*PEOPLE DO GET KILLED DOING this, you know.*

It was seven-thirty in the morning. Scott tried hard to ignore his pounding headache and the knot of fear tightening in his stomach. He was standing in the crowd of lunatics, who were apparently singing some traditional running song. Next to him was an old stone building that had statues on top with what looked like angels wielding clubs. The air was almost sticky with excitement and fear.

Scott was wearing the traditional white shirt, white pants and red handkerchief around his neck. He also had his good running shoes on.

He felt like an idiot. A possibly soon-to-be-dead idiot.

"Whooo! Right *on!*" Finn yelled, bouncing like a six-year-old on a sugar rush. "Are you excited? Are you *pumped?*"

"Are you hungover?" Lincoln asked, at a more normal volume. Finn was surrounded by a bunch of Players, all wearing the white clothes...well, except for Finn, who wasn't wearing a shirt. Finn was self-admittedly "clothing challenged."

"I'm a little hungover," Scott said.

"It'll be fine. It's the people who are still roaring drunk that usually get hurt in this thing," Lincoln said casually, as if he were standing in a drawing room instead of on a cobblestone street in Spain, waiting for some pissed-off, really large bovines to start tearing after him.

"After this, I'm in, right?" Scott said, through gritted teeth. Finn was leading a bunch of the guys in some song in very broken Spanish. From the sound of the crowd, it had a bawdy edge to it.

"You're in like...well, like Finn," Lincoln said with a grin. "Sure you still want it?"

"Would I be here if I didn't?"

Lincoln shrugged. "I think you'll be a good addition, Scott. As long as you're joining for the right reasons."

"What are the—"

Before he could complete the question, there was a shout, and suddenly the crowd went quiet. Tension and anticipation were palpable.

*Oh, crap.* Scott felt adrenaline flood through his system, making him hyperaware. He felt as if his skin was crawling.

"Good luck," a female voice said next to him, and he jumped, startled.

*Amanda.*

He quickly moved her through the crowd, glancing over his shoulder at the guys. "You didn't... I didn't think you were going to run."

"I came all the way to Pamplona," she said, and her voice was filled with that determination that he was starting to realize he totally loved. "I won't just be a spectator. I'd kick myself for the rest of my life."

His mouth went dry as he suddenly got the implication. It was one thing to think of himself possibly dying. But Amanda...

"You've got to get out of here," he said sharply. "Now."

She stared at him, incredulous. "Um, *no*."

"People get killed doing this," he growled.

"Yeah, like you," she said. "So let's just focus and get through this, okay? It'll be a hell of a story."

Anger quickly replaced any nerves he might've had. "Amand..."

Suddenly, a rocket exploded and people started yelling. *"Corre! CORRE!"*

Scott didn't even need the translation. The crowd started moving, white-clad sprinters headed down the uneven streets as the crowd cheered. They'd let out the damned bull.

He started running, jostled by the crowd as they lurched as one headlong down the hill on the uneven street. He wondered if this was what lemmings felt like, just before they found out there was a cliff ahead. He saw Amanda, moving like a gazelle. He felt better being able to see her, and made sure he was close behind. The pace picked up, people yelling. Somebody tripped, almost dragging Amanda with him. Scott caught her and they both jumped over the guy's body, just before he crawled out of the way.

"Oh, my God!" Amanda shouted breathlessly. The crowd was thinning.

"Bull's comin'!" a deep Texas drawl bellowed out, and people pushed to the sides. Scott jumped into one of those little alcoves, grabbing Amanda and pulling her flush against him…just before the biggest frickin' bull he'd ever seen in his life rushed past, like a lumbering freight train that snorted.

"Holy crap!"

Amanda looked at him, fear and exhilaration bright in her eyes. "Oh, my God," she repeated.

*"Run!"* He nudged her, and they started sprinting down the street, amidst the crowd.

The rest of the run was a blur. The ground was uneven and rocky under his feet—it was a miracle he didn't twist an ankle. Thankfully, he'd done some internet research beforehand, had memorized where the turns were. He herded Amanda on the right path. She was graceful, and damned fast.

The bull run was mercifully short, and he saw the end at the Plaza del Toros, a stadium where the bulls would be fighting later that evening. Scott felt a burst of relief when the stadium was in sight. Pouring on one last desperate push of speed, they went through the darkened tunnel and broke out into light.

Scott was in the middle of the stadium, right in the heart of the bullfighting arena. The stands, he noticed, were fully crowded, everyone cheering like mad. He slowed down, walking around the dirt-packed floor of the stadium, stunned by the surreal feeling. This must be what it felt like to go into the World Series, he thought inanely.

"I can't believe that!" Amanda said, as more and more bodies milled around inside the arena floor. It was like a big party—and the spectators were cheering them on like returning, victorious heroes.

He kissed Amanda, holding her against him. "That...was...*incredible.*"

She smiled, holding him fiercely. "Thank you," she breathed. "Thank you for sharing this with me."

He smiled back. "I am going to make love to you all night. And most of tomorrow."

"And then we're..."

"Move it, man!" Finn said as he bolted past them. Then he skidded to a stop. "Who's this?"

"This is Amanda," Scott said, then remembered she was not supposed to know about them, and they probably shouldn't know about her. "She's—"

"Over the wall, Amanda!" Finn said, tugging her arm.

"What?" she asked blankly.

"They're letting 'em in! *Move it!*"

"Letting *who* in?" Scott asked, feeling dumb. Then he glanced back at the tunnel.

The *bulls.* They were letting the bulls in with them!

He didn't know where the energy came from, but suddenly, Scott was chasing Amanda and Finn toward the nearest stadium wall. "What the *hell?*" he shouted, just before boosting Amanda up over the wall. A bull was heading right toward them. Finn skinned up the side of the wall like a squirrel. Scott couldn't get a good hold, and wound up running a little. The bull was distracted for a quick moment.

*Move it!* Scott took a running leap at the wall, felt his fingers connect and clasp around the top. By sheer willpower, he hauled himself up and over, practically feeling the beast's breath against his butt as he did so.

The gathering crowd helped him up, and Amanda was at his side in seconds. Her eyes were wide as dinner plates.

"Congrats!" Finn called, crowing like Peter Pan. "You're *in,* baby! You're *in!*"

"I'm in," he chanted, then looked at Amanda. She was thrilled—it shone on her face. Her confidence and belief in him, her admiration, lit her up like a beacon.

He had everything he wanted. And he was suddenly incredibly glad that she was the one sharing it with him.

"What are you going to do now?" Finn asked, punching him on the shoulder. "We have to celebrate…."

Scott wrapped an arm around Amanda.

"Back to the hotel," he said.

Screw it. He wanted to be a Player—but right now, he wanted Amanda more.

# 12

AMANDA HEARD THE KNOCK on the door first. She rolled over lazily, nudging Scott's nude body. "Room service," she prompted.

He groaned, putting his head in the pillow. "I don't think I can move," his muffled voice replied.

She laughed. "Well, I'm not moving," she answered, yawning and stretching, feeling delicious aches in her well-used muscles. "And I'm hungry."

He turned back to see her, then leaned over, nibbling at her rib cage. "I can take care of that."

"For *food*," she said, laughing, and nudged him a little harder...although, God help her, her body perked up at the low-lidded look of desire in his eyes. "If we keep feeding the other hunger, I'm not going to be able to walk onto the plane to go to Paris."

"So we'll stay here for a few more days." He dipped his head down, pressing a kiss on the top of her breast, then looked up at her like a begging puppy. "I promise I'll make it worth your while."

She was tempted. Tempted to actually pass up a trip

to Paris. *I must be in love.* "Food," she finally forced herself to say, although her voice was breathless.

He smiled at her, shrugging. "Fine. You need to keep your strength up, anyway," he warned, hopping out of bed. "We've still got hours yet before we go to the airport."

She felt like crowing. She was happy. Totally, crazily, unbelievably happy.

He slipped into one of the terry robes, and she tucked herself under the blanket, hoping he got rid of the waiter in a hurry. He opened the door.

"Finn? Lincoln?" Scott said, his tone startled. Then, with an angry undertone, he added, "And *George?* What the hell is this?"

She froze.

"We need to talk to you," George blustered, pushing his way into the room. He caught sight of Amanda, and leered.

"About what?" Scott said, stepping between George and the bed.

"About *her.*"

Lincoln sighed, rubbing his face. "This is stupid, George."

"Yeah, George," Finn said sharply. "It's obvious you've got an ax to grind with him, but this is low, even for you."

"What do you mean, 'even for me'? What's that supposed to mean?" George blustered.

"What are you doing here?" Scott repeated, his voice firm enough to stop the bickering.

George crossed his arms. "We've got *rules,*" he said,

with a slight mocking emphasis. "And the first one is you don't tell. *Anybody.*"

He gestured to Amanda, and she tightened her grip on the blanket, keeping it clutched over her body.

"And you told her."

Amanda blanched. Scott's gaze met hers. Then she stared at George, and at the other men—the one called Lincoln, and the guy she'd met on the run with the bulls, Finn.

"These guys?" she said quietly. "These are your friends?"

"Oh, come off it," George snapped. "You know exactly who the hell we are. You know he's been in The Player's Club."

Her eyes popped wide-open. *Please, please let me be convincing.*

"You're in The *Player's Club?*" she said, and sat up...letting the blanket dip a little before catching it.

As she'd suspected, the George guy was temporarily derailed.

"Well, she knows about it *now*," Scott said. "Which technically means that *you* told her. Does that mean we get to kick *your* dumb ass out?"

Lincoln started laughing, as did Finn. George flushed, scowling.

"So what, you just told her you were running with the bulls? And she believed you?"

"Dude, hundreds of people run with the bulls every year!" Scott yelled. Then he took a deep breath. "You're ridiculous. I did what I needed to do. Now, I've still got a vacation to enjoy, with her."

"No problem," Finn said. "We'll talk later. At the next meeting."

"What about her?" George said. "She *knows!*"

"Yeah, and whose fault is that?" Lincoln snapped.

"Actually, that brings up a point," Scott interrupted. "As long as I'm a full member, I can pledge someone. Right?"

The other men paused in their bickering, looking at him.

"Well, then," Scott said. "I'd like to pledge her."

All three shifted their gaze from Scott to her. Amanda waved weakly, then looked at Scott.

*Maybe now, when I'm naked, isn't the best time for this conversation,* she thought.

George shook his head. "No."

"But she knows. Now, I mean," Scott said, crossing his arms. "And yeah, I'm new, but I think—"

"This has nothing to do with how long you've been a member," George said, laughing. "Do you remember when you showed up? Every meeting you've ever been to? How many *women* have you seen there?"

Scott looked puzzled. The other two guys, Finn and Lincoln, looked embarrassed.

"So what are you saying?" Scott pushed. "No girls allowed? What, are we five?"

"Honestly," Lincoln said, "it's never come up before."

"Yeah, well, it's coming up now," Scott said.

She wanted to cheer. She smiled at him, touched.

"It's not happening," George repeated, sharply. "Finn, you know that you wouldn't get a majority rule on this. No way in *hell*. And we're not just changing the rules because your *boy* here feels like bringing Yoko Ono in."

"Oh, come on," she said, insulted. "I don't even know that I want to join your boys' club if this is the caliber of your membership!"

"Good, 'cause nobody's *asking* you," George said, and Scott shoved him back a step.

"You need to leave," Scott said, murder in his voice.

"You need to *choose,*" George said. "Because I think if we point out that some guy wants to bring his girlfriend on board, how many do you think will go for it? A lot of them join to get *away* from their girlfriends and wives."

Lincoln sighed. "It could cause a dynamics problem," he admitted.

Finn just looked miserable.

"So, what do you say, Scott?" George challenged. "You still in? Or do you need to check with your *girlfriend?*"

She waited. It sucked, but this guy was obviously a moron if he was making demands like this. Well, she'd just try to make it up to Scott. They could have their own adventures.

"I'll talk to you when I get back to the States," Scott said, subdued.

She stared at him as he ushered them out and closed the door behind them.

"What just happened?" she asked, feeling stunned.

"I wasn't expecting any of that," he said, sitting on the bed. "George is a jerk. They're working to get rid of him."

"But…are you still going to join?"

He paused for a long minute. Every ticking second made her feel worse.

"I don't see how it would affect what we have," he said slowly, and her heart fell.

"So you're going to go ahead and join even though they've pretty much said you need to leave me behind," she spelled out.

"I know it meant a lot to you," he countered, sounding defensive. "It means a lot to me, too. I was trying to join before I got together with you."

*Got together.* Just a half-step up from *hooked up* but not quite as classy as *started dating.*

"So does that mean you're dumping me?" he asked caustically.

She blinked. "What?"

"You got together with me so you could join the Club," he said. "So now what? Are you going to stop sleeping with me because they won't let you join?"

Tears welled up in her eyes, but she forced herself to hold them back, taking a deep breath. "Is that how you see me?"

"Isn't that what you did?"

"I did blackmail you to get into the Club," she admitted. "And I apologized, remember?"

"But you've always expected it. Everything you've done to help me has been with that in mind."

She stood up, naked. "Well, Scott, I'm disappointed, but I'm more disappointed that you're going to be okay with them excluding me, treating me like...like some *bimbo.* Do you really expect to have your man club *and* your hot little hookup!"

"You're acting like a jealous, unreasonable *girlfriend,*" he said.

She bit her lip. Felt like an idiot. But at the same time, felt betrayed.

"I don't think it's fair," she said. "That you get to go on all these adventures. And I get to help in the background—or *hear* about them."

"You can find other adventures," he said.

She took a deep breath. Then nodded. "You're absolutely right. I *can* find my own adventures."

"Great." He sounded relieved. "So. Where were we?"

She saw him pat the bed, and blanched. "You. Cannot. Be serious."

"So you *are* punishing me," he accused.

"I'm upset. And you're right about something else—I was acting like a girlfriend," she said. "But I am *not* your girlfriend."

"Do we have to go into that?" he asked. "Why can't we just enjoy the moment?"

*Because I thought I was falling in love with you.* Something about the arrangement stung.

She'd been friends with Ethan, she realized. She'd helped him through business school. She'd helped him when he wanted to start a business, working on Candy-Love with him. She'd been excited…but she'd always been the support. Then he'd fallen in love, gone off, remarried.

She was tired of being the supporting player. And she was tired of being the one who had to "understand" while someone else pursued his dream.

"I'm leaving," she said.

"We don't need to be at the airport for hours."

"No," she said quietly. "I'm going back. To San Francisco. I'm not going to Paris."

He took a deep breath. "Fine. If you really feel that way."

She packed quickly, and got dressed. He watched her, silent, intense. When she got to the door, he put a hand on it, stopping her.

"I didn't know how badly I wanted to be part of this club," he said, his voice pleading for understanding. "I needed a change. Needed an adventure. I was tired of being boring. Damn it, I was tired of being a *nice guy*."

She kissed his cheek. Then nudged his hand away, opening the door.

"I wouldn't worry," she said. "If it's any comfort...I don't think you're a nice guy anymore."

Then she walked out.

# 13

*I DON'T THINK YOU'RE a nice guy anymore.*

Scott rubbed at his eyes with the heels of his palms. Ever since Pamplona, and breaking up with Amanda, he'd felt empty and raw. He'd been to a few Player's Club meetings, but even that had only made him feel worse. Now, he just felt tired, and angry.

"Hey, Ferrell," one of the execs, Charlie, stuck his head into Scott's office. "Some of the guys from Sales are going for drinks after work. Want to come?"

Scott shrugged. A couple of months ago, he would've felt a boost at being included, even though he would've turned it down. Now, he had more social life than he knew what to do with...but he found himself reluctant to drag himself back to his apartment building, knowing Amanda was just a floor away.

"Sure. Why the hell not," Scott said, and Charlie grinned. "Where are we going?"

"We're still figuring that out," Charlie said, frowning. "The guys are saying they want martinis. Know any place?"

"Martuni's," Scott said, then winced, remembering

George and their last conversation there. "Wait…there's a club in the industrial district that I know. Small, private, pretty exclusive."

"How the hell did you get so plugged in?" Charlie said, sounding envious. "You used to be like all the rest of the analysts—you know, quiet, kept your head down, lived and breathed spreadsheets and pie charts. But now there are all these rumors. What *is* going on with you, man?"

"Stereotype much?" Scott asked quietly.

"Huh?"

"Just because we're analysts doesn't mean we're nerds with pocket protectors," Scott said, more weary than bitter. "As far as rumors, I don't know what you're talking about, but I'm pretty sure it's just crap."

"They said you ran with the bulls in Pamplona," Charlie blurted with a dubious laugh.

"All right. That one I did," Scott confirmed. "But so what?"

Charlie's eyes widened, and the laughter died off. "And…you skydived, or something."

Scott shrugged. "Again. So what?"

"And that girl, the one who came by for lunch?" Charlie's mouth dropped. "You *can't* mean that rumor was true. Heard that you guys got busy right here in your office!"

Scott closed his eyes as the heat of that memory seared him right down to the bone. Then he looked right at him, keeping his face completely impassive.

"That's wrong. She was stopping by for lunch. That's it." *Players don't brag,* he reminded himself.

Real players didn't have to.

"Okay," Charlie said, but his tone was tinged with admiration. "Can you send out the directions for... What's the name of this place, anyway?"

Scott wracked his brain. "Speakeasy, I think," he said. "I'll find out."

Charlie left, and Scott focused on his work. Lately, he was either being a party animal or a workaholic, no middle ground. If he only stayed busy enough, maybe the Amanda-size ache in his chest would disappear.

About an hour later, Charlie was back with a few of the other guys from Sales. Scott tried not to look as disgruntled as he felt. "What? You guys missing a report or something?"

"Nah, this is about that club," Charlie said, sounding excited.

"Oh, right." Scott sighed. "I forgot to look up the address."

"No, not *that* club," Charlie said. "The Player's Club!"

Scott gaped. "What?"

One of the guys, Peter, shut the door behind him. "It's all over the internet, came out in the paper. How the *hell* did you get in?"

"And how can you get *me* in?" Charlie tacked on, laughing.

"Wait. Wait," Scott said, feeling like a ball of lead was lodged in his stomach. "What are you talking about?"

Peter rolled his eyes. "Check out the *SF Zine* online."

Scott quickly looked it up, his stomach growing increasingly more queasy. It only got worse as the top headline was Rich, Bored, Living on the Edge: Welcome to The Player's Club.

"So that club you mentioned, Speakeasy," Charlie said, "they've got a picture of that!"

"Oh, crap," Scott breathed, scanning through the article as the other two idiots snickered.

Whoever had written the article obviously had some inside information. There were a couple of shots from Speakeasy, including one of a Bettie Page dancer. Thankfully, it wasn't Amanda. It talked about the hazing, touched on the challenges, but mostly concentrated on the secrecy and the stunts, as well as the drinking, the parties and exclusivity.

It had *George* written all over it. Scott gritted his teeth. If this didn't get him thrown out, then nothing…

Scott stopped as his gaze locked on a sentence in the article, then reread it several times to realize it was indeed there.

> The source, a data analyst for a downtown tech firm who preferred to remain anonymous, had just joined the club after performing a series of challenges—

"Oh, *crap,*" Scott repeated.

It might've been George giving the interview, but whoever it was, was obviously setting him up.

"It is true," Charlie said. "Man. You *gotta* get me in there. How much money do you need?"

"Those dancers looked hot," Peter added. "Can you just bring people to tag along? I'm married, but I could sure use a way to blow off steam."

"Not everybody needs to skydive, though, right?" Charlie asked, worried.

Before Scott could answer, or more to the point kick them out, his cell phone rang. Lincoln's number popped up in the display. Scott answered without even a greeting. "I had nothing to do with this article. I swear."

"Meet us tonight," Lincoln said, his voice arctic. "Down on the wharf, you know the pier. Soon as possible. We're having a meeting."

"More like a lynch mob," Scott surmised. "You know me, Lincoln."

"Do I?"

"I swear. I wouldn't—"

"Just show up." Lincoln hung up on him.

Scott shut off his phone. "Sorry, I can't do drinks tonight."

Charlie and Peter were staring at him. "Was that... *them?*" Charlie asked eagerly.

"Can we come?" Peter begged.

"Okay. Get out!" Scott raged, then got up and grabbed his coat. He'd get over there, fast, and explain. How bad could it be?

*And who did he think he was kidding?*

THE CROWD AT THE IMPROMPTU meeting place—a massive yacht, of all things—showed that Scott wasn't far off with the lynch mob suspicion. They glared at him as he boarded the boat and went into the passenger cabin.

"Let's roll him," one guy, with a tattoo across his throat, said in a growl.

"I'm thinking overboard, out in the Bay," another

guy in a business suit said, and bumped knuckles with the tattoo guy's enthusiastic agreement.

Scott cleared his throat. The normally genial guys of The Player's Club were now assembled around him like a kangaroo court, looking to Lincoln to give them the okay to tar and feather. Unfortunately, Lincoln's grim expression suggested he might give the thumbs-up.

"I didn't give the interview," Scott said emphatically. "You don't have any proof that it was me."

"How many data analysts have joined recently?" Tucker asked caustically. "Oh, wait. *Just you.*"

"It's a setup," Scott retorted. "That wasn't me!"

He waited to see if George would say anything, but for once, the guy was being wisely silent, almost preening with his smugness. George had to be the one behind this. George had never wanted him to join, never liked him—and if Scott became full-fledged, George would find himself with one more person itching to kick him out. It made sense.

Lincoln finally ran a hand over his short-trimmed hair in a frustrated gesture. "We're not going to roll him or throw him overboard," he said, then had to wait a few solid minutes for the furor to die down. "We're not going to punish him."

"What the hell?" a bull-necked guy from George's crew protested. "What kind of wimps are we? We aren't even going to make an example of him?"

"For who?" Lincoln said, and his voice lashed out like a bullwhip. The crowd finally quieted. "He doesn't deserve to be in—I agree with that. I'll make sure he can't get into our databases, he won't know any of our contacts. And I'll put out the word. From here on out, he's not getting in any club in the city. And before you ask," Lincoln added, looking at Scott, "yeah. I can actually do that."

Scott was momentarily stunned, wondering how the hell Lincoln could pull something like that off, but was put off stride when the bull-necked guy walked up to him.

"I'm not going to stand around while this guy breaks the rules," he said, and before Scott could react, the guy's fist was like a cannonball in his gut. He doubled over, gasping for air like a caught fish. He was just getting his breath back when the fist returned, slamming into his cheek and snapping his head to one side. He fell to his knees as pain exploded behind his eye.

He got up, adrenaline flooding him as he lunged at the enormous guy. Before he could land a punch, the Players got between them, Lincoln most prominent.

*"This isn't happening,"* he yelled with that intimidating tone of his. It stalled them, even if both Scott and the big guy struggled against the guys separating them. "Stow this or I swear, The Player's Club disappears. You got that?"

They all turned to stare at him. "Linc?" the bull-necked guy said, sounding shocked.

"The websites, the challenges…the trips, the plans. All of it gone." Lincoln sounded like thunder.

They settled down.

"Time for you to leave," Lincoln said, and escorted Scott to the gang plank. "We're setting sail in a second. Players only."

As they walked toward the deck, Scott dropped

his voice low. "How can you not believe me? It was George. It had to be George."

"George doesn't like me, or what we wanted for this club," Lincoln said, "but even he's not brave enough— or stupid enough—to bring in a reporter. He knows how I feel about it."

Scott clenched his jaw. The side of his face was swelling, and his stomach still hurt. He stepped onto the deck. He stood, staring at Lincoln.

Lincoln simply shook his head. He soon disappeared, and the yacht started to pull away, then picked up speed. Scott watched until it was a dot, far off on the water.

He was hurt. He was pissed. And right now, there was only one person he wanted to talk to. Only one person he really, really needed.

He'd let it go on for too long. He needed to find Amanda, and make things right.

# 14

AFTER DRIVING BACK to the apartment building, Scott steeled himself, then headed up to her apartment. He heard her moving around, then unlatching and unlocking the various locks. When she opened the door, she didn't look angry, at least. Her white-blond hair was in a ponytail, and she was wearing makeup that made her eyes look sultry. "Yes?"

Uh-oh. "Can we talk?"

She sighed. She looked good. No—she looked *great*. She was wearing a dress, something cute and sort of innocent looking, with a pink cardigan sweater. She looked beautiful, and his heart clenched.

"I don't have time to— Oh, my God," she interrupted herself. "What happened to your face?"

He touched his swollen face warily, then winced. "You should see the other guy."

"Really?"

"Yeah. He looks like a goddamned tank," Scott expanded. "Can I come in, please?"

She glanced at her watch. "Just for a second. I'll make you an ice pack."

He walked in. Her apartment smelled like heaven: coffee, cinnamon, chocolate, with the slightest hint of whatever she smelled like—some sexy flower thing. His body responded reflexively, before he could even stop it.

She was putting ice in a plastic bag, and he walked up behind her, stroking her waist, pressing a kiss on her neck even though the side of his lip hurt.

She leaned against him, just for a second. Then she sighed again, turning and handing him the enormous ice bag.

"Put this on," she said. "And you should probably go see a doctor."

"I miss you," he said. He hadn't meant to just blurt that out, but it was too late now.

"Scott, nothing's changed," she said, but her voice was more wistful than mad. "Maybe I overreacted, but honestly, I'm tired of being second place to a man's interests. I wanted an adventure—I got one, and then some. I learned I was more exciting than I thought I was, and I thank you for that. But I'm not going to play second fiddle to The Player's Club."

"But you wouldn't be."

She paused, looking confused. Looking, he realized, hopeful. "You...you gave it up? You walked away?"

"Um..." He cleared his throat. "I'm not in the Club anymore."

She tilted her head. He hadn't lied, but he hadn't exactly volunteered the full truth, either. And she homed in on that fact like a laser.

"What happened?"

"It's not important," he said, even though he wanted

to tell her. He wanted nothing more than to talk to her, ask her opinion, just feel like someone was listening. When he was happy, or when he was unhappy, she was the only person in the world he wanted to talk to. She was sexy as hell, more gutsy and exciting than any ten women he'd met put together. And more than that, she was comfort, and understanding, and…love.

*You love her, you idiot.*

He blinked, and suddenly the punch in the gut was nothing compared to the tight, wind-knocked-out sensation he was experiencing.

"I'm sorry," he said, and meant it. "I'm really sorry. For what I said. For how I acted."

Her eyes got glassy with tears, and she crossed her arms. "You should be. But that doesn't tell me what happened to you and the Club."

He took a deep breath. "There was this newspaper article," he said. "Somebody made it look like I'd talked about the Players."

She stared at him for a long minute. "But you didn't," she said, and there was no doubt in her voice. It was, perhaps, the most gratifying thing he'd ever heard.

"No, I didn't," he said, then gathered her in his arms, holding her tight. "Thank you for believing me."

She nudged him away, gently but firmly. He felt bereft.

"I know it, not just because I believe you, but because I know you wanted to be in that club more than you wanted anything," she said, and there was a touch of bitterness. "You never would've jeopardized that just to brag."

He grimaced. "I probably deserve that. But—"

"They kicked you out," she said. "They think you betrayed them. *That's* how you got punched."

"Basically, yes."

She looked at him, silent, then said, "So you're not here to apologize. You're here because you can't be in the Club anymore, so you're collecting your consolation gift."

"Damn it, that's not it at all."

"I don't have time for this," she said, wiping carefully at her eyes with her fingertips. "I have to go. I have a date."

"We need to talk," he said.

"*No,* we don't." She moved past him, opening the front door. "The worst part is, if I hadn't been so gung ho about this club, so intent on helping you and getting myself in, none of this might've happened. You were stupid, but I let you hurt me."

She gestured to the hallway. "I'm not letting you hurt me again."

"I'm sorry," he said helplessly.

"So am I," she said. "But I'm also late. Good night, Scott."

# 15

LATER THAT NIGHT AT DINNER, Amanda gritted her teeth before she took a sip of water. *Getting back on the horse, getting back on the horse,* she reminded herself. At least, that's what Jackie and Tina had suggested she do, once she'd come home from Spain. She'd first decided to continue and explore Europe on her own. She'd had some delicious food, but instead of comforting her, it had only depressed her more.

"So, what do you do for a living?" Rick, the journalist and coworker that Jackie dug up to be her get-back-on-the-horse date, said with a smile as he started cutting into his steak.

"At the moment, nothing." She poked at her filet mignon. He'd taken her to a steak house, very expensive, very chic. It seemed great. Too bad she wasn't in a red meat frame of mind.

"Nothing?" Rick asked, eyebrows going up. She got the feeling Jackie had been less than forthcoming with details, and he was now wondering if he was having dinner with a loser. Ugh. "Unemployed? Lot of that going around. How's the search going?"

"Lousy." Not that she was actively searching for a job, but the fact that she was without purpose was still bugging her steadily. She ate her scallops. *Overdone,* she thought critically. If there was a next date with this guy, she would choose the restaurant. She knew a great place, hidden adjacent to Union Square, that would put this overpriced joint in the dust.

"What, exactly, are you looking to do?"

She laughed. "That's sort of the problem. I don't know."

"Oh." He took a nervous gulp of his beer. "Hmm. This isn't going very well, is it?"

She frowned. "Sorry. I…just sort of went through a nasty breakup, and I'm trying to get my social skills back."

"Aha." He smiled broadly, leaning back. Like he had her pegged. She went from contrite to annoyed in about five seconds. "Double whammy, huh? Lost your job, and you've got a bad ex-boyfriend. Common story. We write about it all the time, over at the paper."

"Really."

He had that gleam in his eyes, whenever he talked about the stories he worked on. He tried to at least make them entertaining, but they were really a sort of quiet bragging. "Although I write about a lot of fun stuff, too," he continued in a smooth transition. "Did you read the article about The Player's Club?"

She shuddered. "No," she said flatly. "But I heard about it."

"Must be nice, to have all that money to jet around the world, living that death-defying lifestyle," he mused.

She wasn't going to ask, but next thing she knew, the question popped out of her mouth. "So you must've spent time at one of the parties or whatever, huh? Spent time with the guys? Did you do all the crazy stuff with them?"

Now, he squirmed. "I did a lot of research," he said quickly. "There was this other story, about a group of vigilante strippers…"

"So you skydived with them, stuff like that?"

He looked irritated at her persistence. "Well, no. I would've compromised the story if I had tried infiltrating them directly. They're a small group—I would've stuck out."

"You could have joined."

He shrugged. "The paper wouldn't have agreed to that."

She nodded. *Translation: they wouldn't have you.* Scott might have been a lousy liar, but at least he'd tried to avoid lying in the first place. "So you got all your information secondhand," she clarified.

"I had a great source," he defended. "I mean, the guy provided me with pictures, gave me the whole background. I might as well have been there."

"Oh?" Amanda asked carefully, feeling a prickle of reluctant interest. He'd written the story. He knew who the *real* source was. "Why would he agree to talk to you? They're pretty secretive. Did you bribe him or something?"

"Are you kidding? He came to *me*," he said, clearly offended. "He wanted this story done."

Amanda's eyes narrowed. "Since secrecy is one of the top rules…why would he let you print what he did for a living? He had to know that the Club would put two and two together."

"I didn't print his name," Rick snapped. "I kept his anonymity. Besides, he made it sound like the Club was going in a new direction, and they won't care as much about getting into the paper. He could feed me more information."

"I thought that only rich guys were in that club." Amanda didn't know why she was grilling Rick, but she couldn't seem to stop herself. "Was this a rich guy?"

Rick looked a little startled, shaking his head. "You know, I never would've pegged him for a data analyst, actually…not that I know what one looks like, per se. But this guy seemed loaded. Expensive watch, silk tie, the whole nine. I'll bet he bought all that stuff after he joined the Club…" Rick mused, his eyes going hazy. "Well, I'm going to be following up, soon."

"What was his name?"

Rick snapped out of his journalistic reverie. "I protect my sources," he insisted. "Besides, why do you want to know? What's with the police interrogation?"

"I think he's…an old neighbor of mine," Amanda said carefully.

"I can't tell you the guy's name. It would be totally unethical."

"At least describe him to me," she wheedled.

Rick sighed. "Like I said, he looked rich, dressed well."

"Had glasses?" Amanda asked.

Rick smirked. "No. At least, not that I saw. That would've really fit the stereotype, huh?"

"Anything else you can tell me?"

"Well," Rick hesitated, "he did have the reddest hair I'd seen in a while. Now, can we continue with our date? I think your food's getting cold…"

*Red hair.* Suddenly, Amanda remembered George— his smirking, arrogant, repugnant expression as he'd cornered them on the plane, then when he'd tried to intimidate Scott in the hotel room.

Just as Scott suspected: George had set him up. Only now, she had proof.

She pushed her plate aside. She'd lost her appetite. It was Scott's stupid fault they'd broken up, a part of her reasoned. She didn't owe him anything. If he hadn't… If he'd only…

*This still isn't fair. This isn't right.*

She gritted her teeth. "Do you want to go to a Player's Club meeting? For real?"

He blinked at her, and surprised them both when he dropped his fork with a clatter onto his plate. "Seriously?" He was practically out of his seat. "You *know* them? You know how to reach them?"

"I've got some ideas," she said. "But first, there's a guy we need to talk to. Then, we'll head out."

Rick motioned to a waiter, paying in a rush, then all but tugged her out of the restaurant. "What guy are we talking to?"

"An idiot," she replied. "But I love him anyway."

SCOTT SAT IN HIS APARTMENT, drinking a beer and holding the ice bag against his face.

He considered getting even with George. He knew without a doubt that George was the one who had screwed him, and part of him wanted nothing more than revenge. But right now, all he could think about was Amanda. Amanda, the woman he loved.

Who was currently on a date.

He'd been so worried about not being a "nice guy"— so intent on being the badass he thought Amanda wanted—that he'd become the opposite. Selfish, insensitive. Cruel.

No matter what his reasoning, he'd actually treated Amanda poorly. She was right: he'd tried to have his cake and eat it, too. Have The Player's Club, while she waited for him, sharing the adventures he chose to tell her about. Helping *him*. Being there for *him*. Hell, tonight, he'd felt crushed, and he'd gone to her to feel better.

He hadn't even bothered to ask her how *she* was doing.

He was surprised when there was a knock at the door. Cautiously, he glanced around. He figured Lincoln wouldn't put a hit out on him—but there was something really shady about the guy, even if he was really cool.

It was a strange guy. And he recognized Amanda in the fish-eye lens.

He opened the door. "Amanda, I—"

"Scott, meet Rick, my date."

He blinked. Now who was being cruel? "Uh, hi?"

"Great to meet you," the guy said with what appeared to be genuine enthusiasm. He held out his hand. "So, you're in The Player's Club, too?"

"I was," Scott said, shaking hands with the guy. He glared at Amanda. "What's this all about?"

"Didn't I tell you?" Amanda's tone was tart. "Jackie set us up. Rick works with Jackie." She paused a beat. "At the newspaper."

Another journalist, Scott thought, remembering Kayla's date, Matt. Hadn't newspapers gotten him in enough trouble?

"I wrote the article about The Player's Club," Rick supplied helpfully.

"Oh." Then the wheels clicked. "*Oh.* You!"

"Yeah. It was a great article," Rick said modestly. "But more than that...I've been interested in the Club since I first heard about it. That's why I went after the story so hard. I'd give my left nut to join."

"Vivid," Amanda said, wrinkling her nose.

"Very," Scott agreed. "Amanda, can I talk to you alone for a second?"

"All right." She followed him into the kitchen, leaving Rick in the living room. "Scott, he can prove that you weren't the source. What's the problem?"

"You're *dating* him." Scott gritted his teeth. "I know we're not together, whatever. But...why would I help the guy who's dating..."

*The woman I love.*

"You?" he finished.

She rolled her eyes. "This isn't about helping *him,* idiot. This is about helping *you.*"

For the first time that night, he smiled. "Why are you helping me?"

"Because I'm an idiot, too," she said, huffing impatiently. Then she crossed her arms. "I still care about you. You did so much to get into this club. I mean, I just helped, and I couldn't believe what we wound up doing.

What *we* were able to do. Before this, I just worked all the time. I was the dependable one, the boring one. Then I met you, and I heard about the Club, and…and I turned into an exciting burlesque dancer who camps out in the Mojave and runs with the bulls."

For a second, she smiled, too, and it lit her face.

"I like who I am, when I'm with you," she breathed. "More than that, I like knowing I can be myself when I'm with you, whether it's running with the bulls, or just hanging out and watching *Twilight Zone* reruns."

He smiled, reaching for her. "Amanda."

She took a step back. "It's not fair," she said. "You shouldn't have gotten kicked out, and George shouldn't get away with it. I think we should do something about it."

He took her hand. "Thank you."

She gave his fingers a quick squeeze. "It doesn't mean we're…"

"I know," he said softly. "But…if this guy tries to touch you, you realize I'm probably going to kick his ass."

She grinned. "Oh, don't worry. He doesn't have a chance, and even if he did, he'd much rather join the Club than be with me." She paused, laughing humorlessly. "Lotta that going around, actually."

He swallowed hard. "Amanda…"

"Okay, *that* was way more self-pitying than I meant for it to be," she said, scolding herself. She led him back to the living room, where Rick sat up straighter, looking eager. "Come on. Let's go find this club, and let them know what's really going on."

"I don't know how, though," Scott said. "The passwords have all changed. They're not going to answer my calls. How are we going to find them?"

Rick grinned. "Thanks to George, being used has its advantages. I know just how we can find out."

# 16

THE NEXT NIGHT, the three of them were in Rick's black Audi. Scott and Amanda crouched in the back, while Rick read a paper in the driver's seat.

"This is George's house?" Amanda was shocked. "It looks like a mansion."

"It is," Rick replied in a low voice. "He's one of the Macalisters. That's big money."

"Do you think you can follow him without him noticing?" Amanda asked.

Rick shot an irritated look back at her. "I'm a *reporter*. Of course I can."

"George is arrogant," Scott interjected. "I don't think it'll even occur to him to try hiding the fact that he's going to a Player's Club meeting. The guy has stupid business cards showing he's a member, for Pete's sake. He's proud of it."

Sure enough, George came barreling out of his driveway, driving a black Maserati. "That's him."

"Follow that car," Amanda ordered, then giggled. "I've *always* wanted to say that."

Rick followed. "This guy drives like a maniac,"

he groused. "With a lead foot. Keeping up with him might be harder than I thought." He hit the accelerator. Suddenly, they were thrown against the side of the car, Amanda piling onto Scott. She let out a surprised squeal.

"Car chase," Scott said, feeling some laughter bubble up in his chest. This was so crazy.

"Oh, no, you bastard. You're not getting away from me," Rick muttered, and abruptly curved the other way.

"The key is for him not to know we're back here, remember?" Amanda yelped.

"Don't worry! I got him!"

After some more twists and turns, they finally made it to a closed office building. "This?" Rick asked, pulling into the parking garage. "Would the Club meet here?"

"That's his Maserati, right?"

They saw George going up to an elevator, and hid. They followed.

"Elevator's stopping at the fifteenth floor," Scott said, then turned to Amanda and Rick. "You ready for this?"

"She's coming, too?" Rick said, surprised.

"Yes," Amanda said sharply, "*she* is."

"Absolutely," Scott agreed, his heart pounding with every step he took.

AMANDA WAS ANXIOUS, her mind racing as they stepped off the elevators. She could hear voices, male voices, arguing something and see light flooding out of a set of open conference-room doors. Their echoing footsteps weren't heard over the din of the debate.

"I'm telling you, The Player's Club is sick of your rules!" a snide voice shouted. "All in favor of making me leader of The Player's Club, say *'hell, yeah!'*"

"That's it," another male voice said, cutting through the shouting like a scalpel. "George, I've put up with you because Finn is my best friend, and you're his cousin. But you've crossed the line. This isn't a fraternity, and it's not the fucking Moose Lodge. You don't get to be homecoming king because you want to brag about your boozing, and all the women. And you don't get to inflate your ego by hazing guys and then telling them they don't make the cut!"

Amanda stepped in behind Scott and Rick. There were men sitting around in knots, and the two main arguers, Lincoln and George, were standing in the middle, looking as though they were about to throw down and simply slug it out.

She'd have put money on Lincoln. George was heavier, but the expression on Lincoln's face was lethal.

"Excuse me, gentlemen," she said, quietly at first, then raising her voice. *"Excuse me."*

The room fell silent. Clearly stunned, they all stared at her. Amanda felt like shrinking. Instead, she put her chin up, and took a step forward. "I think there's something you need to hear."

"How did you get here?" George said, then took in Scott. "Jesus, Ferrell. You're back? Again? Just begging to get your ass kicked, huh?"

"I'm here to set things straight," Scott defended, refusing to rise to the bait. He wore a smug smile. "I'd also like to introduce someone. His name's Rick, and he's the reporter who wrote the article."

There was a rush of murmurs, and suddenly Lincoln's lethal stare was off the charts. They advanced on Rick.

Rick gulped noticeably, but to his credit, he stayed put. George also paled, she noticed, and she felt a gleeful, evil sense of triumph.

"You want to tell them what you told me?"

"Sure," Rick said, his voice shaking slightly. Then he pointed at George. "He's my source. I've never met Scott before tonight."

The murderous stares shifted to George, who held up his hands.

"This is bullshit," George said, but he stammered, and sweat beaded his forehead. "Scott's got the balls to actually *bring a reporter here.* And you're going to believe him?"

"I didn't have much choice," Scott said. "After you set me up and cut me off. Besides, it wasn't like it was that hard to find you."

"How did you find us?" Finn asked. She'd remembered Finn as a cheerful, vaguely flaky guy. Now, he was stone-cold serious.

"I'm a reporter," Rick said, shrugging, and Amanda groaned softly at the man's arrogance.

"We followed George," Scott added.

Lincoln growled. "Damn it, George…"

"It's him! Why the hell are you mad at me?"

Amanda stepped up. "No, it's *you.* You did it, and now you've been caught. So why don't you stop the crap, and man up already?"

The crowd stared at her. She would've stared at herself if it were possible.

"I like her," Finn said, to no one in particular.

"Me, too," Scott chimed in, grinning.

George seethed. "You can't prove anything."

"You said you want the Club to go in a new direction. Fine. You go in a new direction, and take whoever you want with you," Lincoln announced. "We're through."

"Fine. You guys are a bunch of pussies, anyway," George spat out. "I should've started The Player's Club! Come on, guys. Let's go and really show them what being a Player is."

He headed for the door.

No one followed him.

"Ted? Bulldog?" George said, gesturing for a few guys to leave with him. "What is *wrong* with you guys?"

"That wasn't cool," a huge muscular guy with no neck said. He was wearing a wife-beater shirt, and his bare arms rippled as he bunched his hands into fists. "I hit Scott for something you did. That was a dick move, George."

George took one look at the intent in the guy's eyes...and he ran from the room.

Finn shook his head. "That," he said, "was pathetic."

"Depressing," Lincoln agreed. "Scott, I guess we owe you an apology. But the fact is, you brought a reporter here. And I know you don't know why, but I can't have that. We," he corrected, "can't have that."

Rick stepped forward. "I won't write another article," he said, like a kid begging to stay up. "I just want to be a Player. I'll even tell you if anybody else is writ-

ing anything, or hears anything. I can be helpful. Just…
I want to join."

Lincoln looked at Finn, who grinned. Then Lincoln
grinned, too.

"Okay, Scott," Lincoln drawled. "If everyone else
votes on it, I guess you can be reinstated. All in favor?"

There was a chorus of "ayes." Amanda felt her chest
tighten. She was happy for him. Sad for herself, a little,
but happy for him.

"Thanks, guys," Scott said, when the cheers quieted.
Then, to her shock, he walked over and stood next to
her, taking her hand. "But I'm afraid I'll have to say…
*no.*"

# 17

Scott was watching her face when he turned down the Club. The stunned expression was worth it.

"You don't want to be a Player?" asked Lincoln.

"Oh, I do," Scott said, still not looking away. Amanda's gray eyes were misty and dreamy, staring at him with confusion. "But not without her. She's been amazingly important to me. She's more important than the Club. I finally figured that out."

She smiled, a wobbly, hopeful smile.

"So unless she can join, I'm not in." He tugged her close.

"I might vomit," some guy said, and the bull-necked guy who'd punched Scott glared.

"She's small, but she's tough," the bull-necked guy said. "Why not?"

"I like her," Finn repeated. "I vote yes."

"Me, too," Lincoln said. "All in favor?"

There was another chorus of "ayes." Amanda looked overwhelmed.

"What do you say, Amanda?" Scott asked gently. "Do you want to join the Club?"

She smiled, then nodded. "Yes," she said. "Absolutely yes."

And she squeezed him, hard.

He felt like his chest was going to explode. He looked at Lincoln, who was grinning. "Can we discuss her challenges later?"

"Just don't warn her," Lincoln said.

"I won't." Scott smiled. "We'll see you at the next meeting."

He left Rick talking animatedly to the crew, and hustled her out the door. They caught a cab, and he held her tight the whole way back to the apartment building. They went to her place. He was kissing her before she'd even unlocked the door.

"I missed you," he said. "I screwed up, I'm sorry. God, I'm sorry."

"I love you," she said.

He stopped abruptly, nudging her back. "What was that?"

She looked surprised, like she'd been goosed. "I want to make love to you," she said, shutting the door and reaching for his shirt.

"No," he corrected. "That wasn't it."

She swallowed. "I love you," she repeated softly, but her chin went up, just like it had when she stood up to George.

She was the bravest woman he'd ever met.

He kissed her. "I love you, too," he said, and tasted a salty tear. She laughed against his lips, then held him tight.

"Stay with me," she said.

"Always."

HOURS LATER, THEY WERE on a camping chair on her fire escape at three in the morning—the place where it all started, he joked. She was wrapped in his arms.

"It's getting cool," she murmured, turning on his lap. "We should probably go back inside."

"Not so fast," he said. "We're not finished here."

She chuckled. "What *is* it with you and the great outdoors?" she teased, although she was already going wet with anticipation.

His phone rang. He fished it from the pocket of his jeans, looking at the face of it. "It's Finn," Scott said. "Should I answer it? Or let it go to voice mail? Your call."

She shrugged. "Why not?"

"It'll just take a second," he promised, then opened his cell phone with a click. "Hello?"

She smirked…then reached down, popping open his fly and reaching into his pants.

His eyes bulged, and she laughed softly as she stroked his cock, freeing it from the denim. He frowned at her playfully. "What's up, Finn?"

"I know what's up," Amanda purred as his erection stuck up like a steeple. He bit his lip, his hips arching up toward her. She moved to straddle his thighs, teasing and torturing him.

"Uh…um…yeah. Okay," Scott said, his eyes starting to cross as she leaned down and gave him a quick, careful lick across the tip. She tasted wetness, and went in for a longer suck. "Tomorrow? Right…right… What? Two o'clock? All right." Scott covered the phone with his hand, moaning softly.

Amanda released him, licking her lips. Then she

settled down on top of him, his cock filling her deliciously. She threw back her head, letting her robe fall open to reveal her breasts.

"Listen, Finn, I gotta call you back, man. We'll see you later.... What?" Scott swore. Then he handed the phone to Amanda. "He wants to talk to you."

"Really." Amused, she took the phone, shifting her hips a little so Scott groaned in torment. "Hello, Finn."

"Welcome to the Club, kiddo," he said. "And whatever you're doing to make Scott sound that out of breath—you're a wicked woman. I like that."

She laughed, startled. "Yes, I am." She shivered as Scott pulled her hips, grinding her lower onto him. "And I'm about to be a lot more so, so make it quick."

"Two a.m. at the Factory, okay? I get the feeling Scott was a little too occupied to remember, but I know women are better multitaskers."

She laughed. Then she clicked the phone shut, and tossed it in through the window. "Why do the Players always meet so early in the morning?"

"I don't know," Scott said. "Right now, I don't care. You're the only thing that matters to me."

She smiled. Then she made a soft sound of pleasure as his hands cupped her breasts, urging her forward.

She straddled him carefully as he leaned against the rail. They faced each other, her knees on either side of him. Leaning his head back, he let her set the pace as she rode him there in the open night air, under the stars.

He sat up, his chest pressing against her breasts as she moved her hips more quickly against him. He wound his fingers in her hair as he held her mouth to his, kissing her roughly, passionately. Her breathing was fast, out of control. He was shifting and arching his hips as she thrust downward, urging his cock to slide deeper and deeper inside her.

When the trembling overtook her, she cried out against his mouth. Her body clenched around his, flooding him with her wetness as she shuddered and came. Within minutes, he let out a muffled shout against her lips as he rocked and spasmed beneath her, his orgasm filling her. They collapsed against the back of the padded deck chair. He kissed her sweaty temple, draping her with her discarded robe.

"I love you," he said softly. Solemnly.

She looked deeply into his eyes. "I love you, too."

He made a happy rumbling noise, deep in his chest. Then he glanced at his watch. *"Twilight Zone*'s on in fifteen minutes. I thought we could catch it—unless that's too boring for you now, Ms. Adventurous?"

She winked. "I'll get the hot cocoa going," she said, and kissed him.

# *Epilogue*

AMANDA FELT THE SUN BAKING her like a brick. She absently wiped at her forehead and took a deep breath. Even the air was hot and dusty.

"Just a few more steps," Scott called from behind her, sounding winded.

"Thank God," she said. Then, to her surprise, the satellite phone Lincoln had given her rang. Figuring it was the Club, she answered. "I'm almost there."

"Almost where?" her ex-husband Ethan said, with surprise. "Amanda? Is that you?"

She'd forgotten she had her cell phone forwarded for emergencies. "Are you okay? Something happen?"

"Nothing bad—I was hoping you could watch the store this weekend," he said. "A last-minute opportunity to go to Vegas for the weekend came up, and I was going to take Jillian there for a quick break."

"Sorry. Absolutely can't."

"I was sure you'd be available. Even told her so." He paused. "It's not because you're pissed at me, right? Or her?"

"Not at all," Amanda said. "You know I've never

been spiteful. I'm just… I'm busy myself," she said, as she struggled up another stone step.

"Really?" He sounded amused. "Don't tell me. You've started another business."

"No. Well, not yet," she amended. "I might sometime. Right now, I've just decided to do some things I've always meant to do."

"Well," he said. "I'm impressed. But are you sure you can't take a break in your busy schedule to help out, just this weekend? The manager would do most of the work, but I trust you."

"I really can't," she said with a little laugh. "I'm not even in the country right now."

"You're not?" Now he sounded floored. "Well, where are you?"

She reached the top, taking a deep breath, turning carefully to survey the landscape. Sand and the majesty of the pyramids stretched out beneath her like a postcard. She felt light-headed and triumphant.

"Sorry. Gotta go. Bye!" She hung up. Amanda looked at Scott, who was at her side. "Thank you," she breathed.

"For what?" Scott asked, winded.

She kissed him softly. "For being the best adventure I've ever had."

He smiled back at her, pushing a lock of hair out of her face. "You know what the awesome thing is?"

"What?"

He kissed her, with a bit more intent. "This," he whispered in her ear, "is only the beginning."

\* \* \* \* \*

# PASSION

For a spicier, decidedly hotter read—
this is your destination for romance!

## COMING NEXT MONTH
### AVAILABLE JANUARY 31, 2012

**#663 ONCE UPON A VALENTINE**
*Bedtime Stories*
**Stephanie Bond, Leslie Kelly, Michelle Rowen**

**#664 THE KEEPER**
*Men Out of Uniform*
**Rhonda Nelson**

**#665 CHOOSE ME**
*It's Trading Men!*
**Jo Leigh**

**#666 SEX, LIES AND VALENTINES**
*Undercover Operatives*
**Tawny Weber**

**#667 BRING IT ON**
*Island Nights*
**Kira Sinclair**

**#668 THE PLAYER'S CLUB: LINCOLN**
*The Player's Club*
**Cathy Yardley**

HBCNM0112

# REQUEST YOUR FREE BOOKS!
## 2 FREE NOVELS PLUS 2 FREE GIFTS!

### Harlequin *Blaze*
### red-hot reads!

**YES!** Please send me 2 FREE Harlequin® Blaze™ novels and my 2 FREE gifts (gifts are worth about $10). After receiving them, if I don't wish to receive any more books, I can return the shipping statement marked "cancel." If I don't cancel, I will receive 6 brand-new novels every month and be billed just $4.49 per book in the U.S. or $4.96 per book in Canada. That's a saving of at least 14% off the cover price. It's quite a bargain. Shipping and handling is just 50¢ per book in the U.S. and 75¢ per book in Canada.* I understand that accepting the 2 free books and gifts places me under no obligation to buy anything. I can always return a shipment and cancel at any time. Even if I never buy another book, the two free books and gifts are mine to keep forever.

151/351 HDN FEQE

| | | |
|---|---|---|
| Name | (PLEASE PRINT) | |
| Address | | Apt. # |
| City | State/Prov. | Zip/Postal Code |

Signature (if under 18, a parent or guardian must sign)

Mail to the **Reader Service:**
**IN U.S.A.:** P.O. Box 1867, Buffalo, NY 14240-1867
**IN CANADA:** P.O. Box 609, Fort Erie, Ontario L2A 5X3

Not valid for current subscribers to Harlequin Blaze books.

**Want to try two free books from another line?
Call 1-800-873-8635 or visit www.ReaderService.com.**

\* Terms and prices subject to change without notice. Prices do not include applicable taxes. Sales tax applicable in N.Y. Canadian residents will be charged applicable taxes. Offer not valid in Quebec. This offer is limited to one order per household. All orders subject to credit approval. Credit or debit balances in a customer's account(s) may be offset by any other outstanding balance owed by or to the customer. Please allow 4 to 6 weeks for delivery. Offer available while quantities last.

**Your Privacy**—The Reader Service is committed to protecting your privacy. Our Privacy Policy is available online at www.ReaderService.com or upon request from the Reader Service.

We make a portion of our mailing list available to reputable third parties that offer products we believe may interest you. If you prefer that we not exchange your name with third parties, or if you wish to clarify or modify your communication preferences, please visit us at www.ReaderService.com/consumerschoice or write to us at Reader Service Preference Service, P.O. Box 9062, Buffalo, NY 14269. Include your complete name and address.

HBI1B

# Rhonda Nelson

**SIZZLES WITH ANOTHER INSTALLMENT OF**

Men Out of Uniform

When former ranger Jack Martin is assigned to
provide security to Mariette Levine, a local pastry
chef, he believes this will be an open-and-shut case.
Yet the danger becomes all too real when Mariette is
attacked. But things aren't always what they seem,
and soon Jack's protective instincts demand he save
the woman he is quickly falling for.

## THE KEEPER

**Available February 2012
wherever books are sold.**

*Louisa Morgan loves being around children.*
*So when she has the opportunity to tutor bedridden Ellie,*
*she's determined to bring joy back into the motherless*
*girl's world. Can she also help Ellie's father open his*
*heart again? Read on for a sneak peek of*

### THE COWBOY FATHER

*by Linda Ford,*
*available February 2012 from Love Inspired Historical.*

Why had Louisa thought she could do this job? A bubble of self-pity whispered she was totally useless, but Louisa ignored it. She wasn't useless. She could help Ellie if the child allowed it.

Emmet walked her out, waiting until they were out of earshot to speak. "I sense you and Ellie are not getting along."

"Ellie has lost her freedom. On top of that, everything is new. Familiar things are gone. Her only defense is to exert what little independence she has left. I believe she will soon tire of it and find there are more enjoyable ways to pass the time."

He looked doubtful. Louisa feared he would tell her not to return. But after several seconds' consideration, he sighed heavily. "You're right about one thing. She's lost everything. She can hardly be blamed for feeling out of sorts."

"She hasn't lost everything, though." Her words were quiet, coming from a place full of certainty that Emmet was more than enough for this child. "She has you."

"She'll always have me. As long as I live." He clenched his fists. "And I fully intend to raise her in such a way that even if something happened to me, she would never feel like I was gone. I'd be in her thoughts and in her actions every day."

Peace filled Louisa. "Exactly what my father did."

Their gazes connected, forged a single thought about fathers and daughters…how each needed the other. How sweet the relationship was.

Louisa tipped her head away first. "I'll see you tomorrow."

Emmet nodded. "Until tomorrow then."

She climbed behind the wheel of their automobile and turned toward home. She admired Emmet's devotion to his child. It reminded her of the love her own father had lavished on Louisa and her sisters. Louisa smiled as fond memories of her father filled her thoughts. Ellie was a fortunate child to know such love.

*Louisa understands what both father and daughter are going through. Will her compassion help them heal—and form a new family? Find out in*
*THE COWBOY FATHER*
*by Linda Ford, available February 14, 2012.*

**Love Inspired Books celebrates 15 years of inspirational romance in 2012! February puts the spotlight on Love Inspired Historical, with each book celebrating family and the special place it has in our hearts. Be sure to pick up all four Love Inspired Historical stories, available February 14, wherever books are sold.**

USA TODAY bestselling author

# Sarah Morgan

brings readers another enchanting story

# ONCE A FERRARA WIFE...

When Laurel Ferrara is summoned back to Sicily
by her estranged husband, billionaire
Cristiano Ferrara, Laurel knows things are about
to heat up. And Cristiano's power is a potent
reminder of his Sicilian dynasty's unbreakable rule:
once a Ferrara wife, always a Ferrara wife....

**Sparks fly this February**

Discover a touching new trilogy from
*USA TODAY* bestselling author

# Janice Kay Johnson

## Between Love and Duty

As the eldest brother of three, Duncan MacLachlan
is used to being in control and maintaining an
emotional distance; as a police captain it's his job.
But when he meets Jane Brooks, Duncan soon finds
his control slipping away. Together, they fight for a
young boy's future, and soon Duncan finds himself
hoping to build a future with Jane.

*Available February 2012*

## From Father to Son
*(March 2012)*

## The Call of Bravery
*(April 2012)*

HSR71758